ROSE WIELDER

ROSE WIELDER

T. R. PERRY

t.r.perrywrites

Contents

Preface

Hello, my readers! Thank you for reading this!! Check out my website at **trperrywrites.net** and follow me on Instagram and YouTube **@trperrywrites** so you can get the latest updates on new books.

A few notes before we start this journey together. So, I am from the United States Virgin Islands. This is where my family is from, so I have spent so, so much time there and it just runs through my veins. I wanted to use my experiences growing up between cultures of mainstream America, black America, and Caribbean cultures to inspire the struggles faced throughout the story. It's quite interesting what happens when you get a bunch of cultures together and mix them up to see what happens.

Okay, secondly, the language used in this book was created by me. I majored in Linguistics during college, so I wanted to use this background to help me make something fun. Please remember that I literally made this up, so please do not worry if it means something in another language. That was 100% *not* my intention. What my intention *was* is as follows: 1) I am a big nerd when it comes to J.R.R. Tolkien and his books *The Hobbit* and *Lord of the Rings*. So for me, I just really wanted some sort of language like he had. It's always been a dream for me since I accidentally deciphered the alphabet used in the Hobbit... a story for another day, haha. 2) I wanted to find a way to capture what I experience on a regular basis as being part of a Caribbean family. In the US and British Caribbean islands, there are

English words primarily, but then there are other words that are sort of... a mix of many languages. Because those areas were conquered by the Dutch, French, Spanish, and more at various times, Creole dialects began forming mixing bits of those languages together. What's cool is that there are Caribbean words I know that most of my American friends don't. Therefore, I wanted to capture this spirit of having Caribbean words that most people don't understand but are a big part of your vocabulary. Therefore, I made up my own to try to capture this sentiment.

Acknowledgements

Okay, so this is a really cool thing I've always wanted to do. I just wanted to thank all those awesome people that helped make this book possible.

First, I thank GOD IN HEAVEN, because God and I both know that he is the one who believes in me and my ability to do this. Thank you God for putting these stories in me and helping me to make a really big dream come true!

Second, I have to thank my family. They were literally so kind to me and my ultimate hype squad as I started my journey on this book writing thing. Madre, thank you for reading to me since I was a baby so I would have such a strange affinity for words. Daddy, thank you for just being all calm and always believing I would do great things. I don't know why, but I feel like you just always expected this, and that does wonders for me, honestly. Stepdaddy, I love so much how you just unexpectedly are super extra and super opinionated, and how you help me laugh when I feel stressed. Stepmadre, thank you for your support of just looking at the products, being impressed generally and always being so impressed in this journey. Lil bro and lil sis, you guys are so fun and funny and the best siblings I could have. You have great imaginations and the ways you look up to me inspires me to be a better older sister to you both. And G.S. Carr is my cousin, y'all! Go check her out and her romance novels. She really helped me out with the nitty gritty of how to plot a book in the first place and she explained to me how to use Amazon for publishing. She's great, thank you so much!!

Okay Jam, now's your time to shine. I should honestly write a whole blog or make a video about this, but my sister Jam is probably the one to blame for all of this book stuff anyway. See, before I was writing *this* book, I found an old story from when she and I shared a gmail account as kids and I was *convinced* that it was a short story I had written. I was so fired up that I decided to continue it and turn it into a novel. It wasn't until I wrote four chapters of writing that she told me it was actually *her* story... Guys, I was so bummed about this. All this time I thought I was such a cool writer and it was her idea! The truth is that she's way cooler than me in most ways, but you won't know that since you're just reading my book, hehe. Maybe one day she'll let me finish it, and if so, I'll be sure to let you know. Anyway, that situation lit a fire under me like no other. I realized I couldn't go on without writing a book. I was already in the headspace. So, I got a fresh piece of paper, brainstormed wildly and started writing. And so, here we are today. So Jam, thanks for pushing me to get my *own* story, for keeping me company while I wrote since I like people, for reading my first drafts and being so silly and believing in me all the time.

Now on to my beta readers. Listen, these guys are AWESOME, and I am so *so* grateful for all of them!! Giving you my second draft really made me realize how real all of this was. And your thoughtful and kind words of advice, your ideas for making the plot juicy, and your enthusiasm all were crazy heart-warming. Like, I realized that I was actually writing something that made *somebody* want to read it, and this helped me to believe that others would want to as well.

And finally, I need to thank Covid-19. Yes, you heard it right, folks. I have to thank the 2020 pandemic. This thing slowed the whole world down. And as I sat at home for the first time in years doing online classes, being distraught by racial injustice, and also doing a whole lot of nothing, I realized something. I realized that we don't really know what's going to happen tomorrow, and therefore, if I had a dream to write a book someday, I had better write it as soon as possible. There was no guarantee that tomorrow was going to look anything like I expected. So yes, thank you Covid for giving me the space and the mental clarity to realize I needed to write NOW. And also, the climate that Covid created allowed all of us to stop and pause and behold the racial injustice that was always there. I was never the silent type, but I realized I needed to do more. I needed to write something to be a story for those of us in the dark, in the shadows of mainstream cultures, for the minorities who face injustice all day long. Maybe I couldn't be a lawyer or a politician or a preacher, but I could surely write books.

With that, enjoy, friends.

Apprenticeship

"No! Please, Sir! Stop!" I struggled against his grip, but he was too strong for me. Blackness surrounded me, forcing me to breathe its thick darkness. We inched closer to the rocky edge.

"Quiet, Mello!" he answered gruffly. Still holding my arm firmly, he used his other to pull something out of his cloak. A dagger shone in his fist through the dark night. Wind whipped around us violently, my hair slapping me painfully in my cheeks as it pulled his cloak in multiple directions.

"Let me go, let me GO!" Ignoring my desperate screams, he steadied himself to deal the deathly blow, but quickly whipped his head around when he heard voices behind him.

"Looks like you'll get away this time, *Princess*," he muttered through clenched teeth.

"BUT YOU WON'T!" I screamed back. Closing my eyes, I concentrated, letting heat well inside. Iridescent rays shot from my hands to his hairy arms and he cried out in pain. He fell off the cliff, still writhing as he went, but the power coming out of me made me drop to my knees, into blackness.

Startled, I opened my eyes, letting soft rays of light fall into my chamber. Closing them again, I drew in a deep breath and let it out, fighting against my quickly beating heart. *It's just a stupid dream,* I told myself. Immediately, I heard a ringing bell from my maid, Anne.

"Arabella, your bath is ready!" she called out impatiently. Slowly, I rose up and sauntered to the wash chamber. Quietly, my women finished their task. Once they dressed me, I began the long walk to the breakfast chamber... whiiiichunfortunately involves interacting with my parents, or more specifically, with my mother. The train of my golden gown weighed me down from behind. Rolling my eyes, I grabbed heaping folds of fabric, steadying them in my arms as I walked. *Much better,* I decided, grinning. Pleased with myself, I waddled the rest of the way down the hall.

Goodness, didn't they stop to think about us short legged folk when making these things? Certainly not everyone could have the same shape here. That was one thing I hated about these dresses— they always fit in all the wrong places, made for an average Promynthian body. I guess I just didn't have whatever they were expecting from their other princesses? Well, I definitely was not like Mother for sure, all tall and shapely. I was more of a small stick shape, just a short thin rectangle, like a biscuit. *You'll grow into it,* Mother would always say with a reassuring smile. I pursed my lips in disappointment. Somehow, I knew I never would.

In any case, I triumphantly burst into the breakfast chamber, proud of my newfound dress hack. Cheesing brilliantly,

I curtsied at my parents, still holding the fabric between my arms, ignoring Mother's eyebrows judging my genius. "Good morning, Dear," Father said with a smile, clearing his throat to disguise his laughter.

"Hello, Father," I said back, before jumping into his arms gleefully. I always appreciated his strong frame holding me close. I fit so well in his arms. He placed his hands softly on my shoulders, planting a kiss atop my head. Yeah, Father was great. It was *Mother* who made me nervous, what with her constant questioning and expecting me to be perfect and all. Glancing at her behind Father, I nervously smoothed my dress from my waist to my skirt, hoping that I wouldn't have too much of a crease in it and that I would appear normal and not disturbed from my recurring dream.

Unfortunately, she saw right through my act. "What's troubling you, Dear?" She had already started eating, but paused to gaze at me with concerned, brown eyes staring intently into the depths of my soul. That was one thing. Even though she's really tough, I also know she cares so much for me. It's just that, I can tell she expects a lot, and that's way too much pressure. I feel like she just wants me to become her, which I knew I could never do. Her presence alone is at once breathtaking and majestic, her straightened hair heaped daringly atop her head, powdered face bright and fair.

"Nothing, Mother, just the usual dreams," I lied, shrugging.

"Have you been using your medicines?" There was silence from me. Of course not— they always made me feel weird anyway. "You know you must use them to sleep well, Arabella," she reminded me solemnly.

"Yes, Mother, I know." Hoping to change the subject, I

joined them to eat. Our servants set before us a beautiful array of fine fruits, exotic meats, and sweet breads, as usual. My favorite part included the small cakes and cinnamon tea. We always eat to the sound of my favorite music, the mandolin, which, for some reason, resonates with a deep part of me somewhere. As I got myself a second helping of tea, my father took a deep breath as if to speak. My heart began to race in anticipation and curiosity.

"Arabella?"

"Yes, Father?"

"Mother and I have important news for you."

"What is it?" I asked, trying to mask the intrigue in my voice.

"We have been developing a wonderful opportunity for you," he began. I swallowed hard, looking down for a moment to catch myself. Would I be able to succeed? To please Mother? Seeing my uneasy silence, he added, "We have decided it is time for you to begin your apprenticeship."

"Apprenticeship?" I looked at him, my wide eyes betraying both my nervousness and excitement.

He continued. "Promynthia is a country built on unity, as you know, and we have some areas that aren't exactly cooperating with that objective—"

Mother finished for him. "So, we're assigning you to Melinda to get them to stop being so isolated." My heart fluttered. I wanted nothing more than to go out and do something for once. I honestly hadn't left the castle without my parents since I was a little girl. And even then, I would spend most of my time indoors or waving briefly from a well-padded carriage.

"See, she is smiling, Dear. I knew she would be happy," Mother added as she reached across the table for Father's arm. I half-smiled at that. They did have a great connection. Considering how differently they looked and grew up, I appreciated how they had come together in marriage to lead the whole kingdom. It gave me hope that maybe someday I, too, could find someone to love me.

"But, Arabella, you must know that you cannot do this without direction," Father added earnestly and with a light chuckle.

"Of course," I agreed, nodding back.

"The apprenticeship is designed to give you that direction and supervision whilst you do your independent program," he continued.

"That seems nice."

"Yes," Mother agreed. "It is a new initiative where we've organized the heirs of the various provincial officials across our empire to give each of you an opportunity to learn your trade."

"And to collaborate amongst yourselves," Father added. "It was actually your Uncle Jacob's idea," he added, shrugging. "We were just the official stamps!" I raised my eyebrows. So this *was* legitimate— a real opportunity to finally get out of the house and figure out how to do this ruling thing. I felt a bit warm inside, and not just from the eggs in my stomach. If my parents were letting me do this, maybe it meant that they were finally starting to trust me. I mean, I *was* sixteen, after all. They couldn't keep me hidden in the castle forever. Right?

"And," Mother added slyly, "You could find yourself the next king of Promynthia." Warm feeling over.

"I don't know about that, Mother," I squeaked, my face turning red.

Her mouth curled in response as she looked me up and down, "And why not? With my genes you could do just about—"

"I just can't say I can plan that sort of thing!"

"But *we* can," she declared. "Certainly, we could always Arrange Something—"

But I cut her off again. "Nope! I think I will be just fine." I pushed myself away from the table, then, curtsying and exiting the chamber, ignoring their surprised faces. Conversation averted. Closing my eyes and pausing for a moment, I took a deep breath. I had made it out alive.

Quickly, I grabbed my mandolin from its familiar hook on the wall near the door and ran outside to the pavilion. The outside air was a welcome change to the stuffy, dusty indoors. The warm air brushed softly against my face and skin, heating my insides as well. I strolled to the pavilion, which lay out on the green plain, elevated and connected by a thin, white dock. Not a moment after getting out there, I took off my outer gold skirt. It was actually more of a clip-on (thanks to a secret agreement I made with the seamstresses). Relieved, I left it behind to reveal a calf-length, flowing cream colored skirt. Feeling lighter, I relaxed, curling up on the pavilion bench and releasing my brown curls from their tight prison atop my head. I was glad to set them free and feel them follow gravity's course down my shoulders. My hair wasn't straightened like Mother's. I guess it just seemed like too much work. Besides, I liked the curls. They made me feel different. The only price was that I had to wear my hair in a bun with an ungodly amount of gel for any formal event, including breakfast. Happily, I shook my mane free, refreshing my curls with my fingers to return them to their usual bounce.

The gazebo was perfect. It was its own little, painted island in the whole field of grass, and there was a colorful flower garden that surrounded it as well. Even better, roses and ivy vines wrapped themselves beautifully around the columns of my sanctuary. I, too, felt wrapped in their beauty as I held tight onto my instrument. Feeling playful, I picked some of the pink roses down and, using the long stems, wove them together like a crown on my head— a much better tiara in my opinion than whatever they would be giving me eventually. I began to pluck and sing softly to a tune that I knew from somewhere deep in my soul. Feelings of familiarity and peace swelled in my chest as my heart swayed to its sound. I honestly didn't even know what the language was:

Qua ye ye tuti mana
You are one of a kind, my darling
Sho ni tu faya orli
And safe and warm you will stay

Not wanting the moment to end, I extended the notes with new melodies, always adding a little more to my song, or perhaps creating new strumming pattern. I continued out there for at least an hour. And when I could no longer think of a song, I just sat there, closing my eyes and breathing in the wind.

Satisfied, I eventually returned to my room to nap. The sun is both life-giving and draining, yet I loved it all the same. I plopped onto my bed and was immediately asleep. A knock at my door from Anne woke me up sooner than I would have hoped.

"The Queen requests your presence, Princess," she squeaked. I hurried out of bed and frantically began to powder myself. I figured it would help hide the deepening of my complexion from my sun excursion. Of course, Mother is always trying to wipe away bit of my identity, even right off my skin. I had scarcely put it away and plopped my hair into a messy bun when—

"Arabella Bysentor, what is taking you so long?"

"I have been sleeping, my Queen," I stated, more calmly than I felt, trying to hide the heaving of my breath from moving so fast. "Forgive me," I added, curtsying for extra effect.

She rolled her eyes and folded her arms impatiently. "We have yet to discuss the other part of your apprenticeship, Daughter."

"Other part?"

"Yes." She paused, waiting for my breath to slow down so I could listen carefully. "Once you are successful in your task, you will be coronated officially into your full duty in the kingdom," she explained. My mouth dropped. "Mother, I—"

"I know it is much sooner than we had been preparing for. But your father and I see this as an incredible opportunity and do not want to let it pass. We see the kingdom as ready for your influence, Dear. And, the state of the Melindan island has only grown worse. People there are dissatisfied with their rags, restless with their sentencing to that island, even treasonous about it. Your uncle has kept us informed with his own army that regularly walks the premises. He says people are even wanting to attack the palace with their dark magic!"

I squinted my eyes at her in disbelief. *Really Mom? "Dark magic?"* I thought. That sounded like some kind of stupid fairytale. "You don't really believe those fables, do you, Mother?"

"Of course not!" she snapped more quickly than necessary. Then, clearing her throat and adjusting the folds of her collar, she added, "But, nonetheless, the sentiment of disloyalty remains. For the continuation of Promynthia as a unified people, we must quickly improve the situation there, and see you as the perfect one to do so." I rolled my eyes. Of course, I was the one they'd use. Being black is always a problem until they need to use you as some token child to communicate with the other brownies. "And after you succeed, your father and I see no reason to wait."

I looked down. I certainly saw reasons to wait, including my height, relationship status, and skin color, yet I saw no point in arguing. "Yes, my Queen," I whispered.

"Daughter?"

I lifted my eyes to meet my mother's for a moment. "Yes, Mother?"

"If you should fail your task to improve Melinda, we will have no choice but to... repurpose the lands." She looked almost in pain, standing stiffly and allowing those last few words to land against my ears.

"Repurpose? But where will the people living there go?"

"They will have to find other homes I suppose," she said coldly.

I looked her up and down in disgust. "You would uproot your own people in the name of 'unity'?"

"*My* people," she stated with a low, steady voice, "are those of Promynthia, and our duty is to bring them peace. If the Melindians cannot become like *us*, they will have no choice but to find shelter elsewhere."

"What even are we, Mother?" I breathed. Steadily and with anger burning in me enough to burn, I gazed upon the powdered corpse that had long ago replaced her vibrancy.

"I am the queen," she stated, yet her voice faltered. Struggling to gain control against tears beginning to swell in her eyes, she cleared her throat and added just above a whisper, "We will ready you for your apprenticeship. Do not fail your task." She swiftly exited, closing the door behind her. I threw my pillow at the door in disgust.

2

Beginning

Against my will, we started for the castle the following morning. They really wasted no time with this apprenticeship, I guess. It was only an hour west of us, which was a nice surprise, for sure. It gets way too cramped in there after about two hours, and the horses, bred for speed and steadiness, would make our trip even more comfortable. Thankfully, my parents would be in a separate coach than me, so I wouldn't have to be so... proper.

Waking up that morning was certainly a drag, but there was also some part of me that felt hopeful. Maybe if I could get this thing right, then I'd actually be useful for something. But of course, that light feeling would be tested by the long hallway walk to the door. Gathering my skirts in my new-fangled technique, I started my mini journey.

In the hallway, portraits of my family line, ordered chronologically from the beginning of our history until now stared at me as I passed by. These are the great rulers I knew I had to be like someday. Right by my door was General Edward Bysentor I, or Great Great Great Great... (you get the point, sorry I always lose count here) Grandaddy.

At the beginning of our great reign, he led the ambush of a neighboring country, Melinda, that threatened our own land's prosperity with their dark arts. But obviously that wouldn't be "magic" or anything, it's more of an exaggeration of their excellent warfare skills. I tell you, Promynthians use any excuse they can to discredit the great work of dark-skinned people, even resorting to something as silly as magic! I shook my head.

In an act of mercy, however, Great (times three hundred years of generations) Granddaddy worked with the Melindanking to create terms of peace. Instead of killing them all, the Melindans became citizens of Promynthia. Their old land doubled the size of our own land. The peace he created earned him the throne, and our family has been in power ever since. At some point, the people became too "unruly," as they told me. So, they were relocated to that island in the province of Walabe and have been quarantined there for a hundred years. I guessed that's where I would be heading for this apprenticeship.

As I passed by Granddaddy, I almost caught him looking down smugly at me. It was almost like I could hear him saying, "What's the matter, girl? Can't sacrifice a silly people for your own greatness? You know you're not really one of them. Do it for the crown." I questioned myself too. *What in the world was I supposed to do to prove my worth to our kingdom? And what lengths did I have to go to do so?* I shuddered at that thought, hurrying down the rest of the hall, passing by the rest of the portraits.

Every Bysentor has continued to increase our name. Each picture showed a royal succeeding their formers with greater acts of mercy, kindness, and most importantly, power. We extended our mission of "correcting," slowly turning country after country to our more profitable rule, until we became an empire. Each face fit perfectly into the rectangular frame fashioned for it. By tradition, they won't paint mine until I demonstrate my own of mercy. *Well, we'll see how that goes.*

My parents' picture was at the end of the hall right by the door. Mother's likeness stands out from the rest, and not just because of her surpassing beauty and grace. Father began a new wave of peace where he is trying to bring the provinces together more. Each used to be its own nation, so naturally they're more divided and set in their own ways. His vision is to help them feel as if they are all part of one big whole. I began smiling softly as I reflected on Father. He was always trying to bring people together, even me and Mother. This is probably why they started the apprenticeship process in the first place, to try to bring the different people together, from the noble's kids on up.

What's most impressive about my father is that he didn't just talk the part, but he lived it out. When it came time for his act of mercy, he chose to marry my mom, a poor Melindan girl living on the streets of the quarantined island. I think he figured by beginning with the original enemy and marrying her, that he could show our people that Melindians and our provincial peoples are just like the rest of us, promynthian at heart. That's our country's motto.

For some reason, though, chills ran up and down my spine as I passed by them and left the palace. I guess I was just stuck comparing Mother's and Father's skin tones. She is in such sharp contrast to the rest of our line, needless to say. I looked down at my own caramel-colored hands in distress, wondering if I would ever be seen as truly Promynthian enough. Enough to be a legitimate ruler. With those thoughts, I swiftly entered my coach and drifted off to sleep, which was probably the best thing I could do for my nerves.

I dreamt that I wasn't royal at all and instead could my mandolin all day. But then, as I was playing, a figure in a white coat multiplied all around me. Frightened by his presence, my hands became extremely warm, and suddenly, my mandolin was on fire in my hands! I threw it at the figure but missed him. Then, I was surrounded by flames! I awoke with a start and began rubbing my temples. I wondered if I had remembered to pack my oils. That always took away the stressful dreams. Honestly, it was almost like those serums were suppressing some inner part of me when I took them, like I was suffocating something deep inside. *But that's crazy, right?*

My thoughts were interrupted by the realization that the coach was slowing to a stop. I guess we had arrived at my uncle's Dome. A few minutes later, a servant swung the door open before me. Warm rays reached out for me. Something in me wanted to reach back, but I fought the urge, remembering Mother's rule. Instead, I put on my gloves as I had been taught. A servant had already unfolded my umbrella for me and held it in place, a laced ceiling I could not rise above.

Mother and Father had just arrived as well. As they led our entourage, with the guards and servants flanking us, we had nothing short of a small army escorting us into the Dome of Cyrote. This was where the sons and daughters of the provincial leaders, as well as I, would be meeting for our apprenticeship. I pulled my gloves tighter on my hands as we walked.

Finally, we were safe inside. I looked up, eyeing the large glass case above us. The entire main structure was circular, with white walls surrounding us and black, speckled marble gracing the floor. The ceiling, however, was made completely of thick, sparkling glass that scattered the light inside until it flooded brilliantly into the palace.

"You will be wonderful, Arabella," Father beamed once we stopped right outside the room for our class.

"I expect nothing less," Mother cooed in a low voice. I curtsied to them and took my servant's arm. I knew I would see them in three months, but I still felt a little pang of sadness. Would they miss me? And then even more fears crept in. I would be living with these other provincial heirs, no doubt snobby even though they weren't even high royalty. *What would they think of me and my... um, Melindan-ness?*

"Are you ready, Princess?" my servant asked, interrupting my insecurity.

"Yes, Julian, thank you," I replied, masking my feelings and the truth that I would probably never be ready for this. He bowed to me warmly, offered his arm, and led me into the conference room where the heirs waited eagerly for my arrival. He took my gloved hand into his own and kissed it for extra luck, bowing again and never letting his eyes stray from mine. I smiled faintly. Julian, warm and wise, about my father's age, was my kindest servant. He had served me from my youth, half-Melindian himself and outcasted by others. We took him in because my parents figured he would be a great comfort to me. At least they were right about something.

I took a deep breath just before entering to get my bearings and smiled at Julian for extra support. Surely, I would not be what they expected. With me entering the room, all conversation came to a hush and nineteen bright faces locked their gazes on me.

The 20th face, my uncle, smiled politely at me.

"Dear Princess!" He bowed low, his long robes beginning to gather on the ground. "Welcome to my palace, the Dome of Cyrote." Some students began whispering, realizing that I was the princess. As he rose from his dramatic bowing, he firmly readjusted the grand golden hat he wore atop his head. It flopped to the back of his head as it was quite long. Then, he made sure to grab his long staff for extra support. He'd had a limp in his leg for years.

"Thank you, Uncle," I replied with a regal smile.

"Now," he added, looking out expectantly towards the entrance, "Where are that king and queen of yours?"

"Jacob!" my father burst through the door suddenly. I guess they weren't leaving quite yet. Although I noticed Mother stayed in the hallway. It was probably for the best. Too many Melindans in one room probably caused uncomfortability. She knew how to play the game.

Father let out a deep chuckle and embraced his brother, their robes tangling in a massive, expensive heap. Then, turning towards me, Father held my hand, beaming. "This is my daughter, Princess Arabella Bysentor." I smiled again at my uncle awkwardly, trying to ignore the obviousness of the declaration. "Isn't she just stunning?" he added. *Aw, so sweet, Father!*

"Yes! She is rather something, isn't she!" Uncle replied. I scrunched my eyebrows. *What is that supposed to mean?* But I brushed his comment off quickly, deciding it must be well meaning. His kindness, though a little fake was nice. And besides, it was time to represent the crown and my family, not worry over frivolous comments. Yet, faithful Julian, sensing my discomfort, quickly led me to my seat in the front row before exiting the room. My face began turning reddish as I realized that the other nobles had been staring at us the entire time.

That's when Father turned to address the class. I might have died in that moment, wishing he would go away so I could blend into the others. (Although that was pretty hard considering skin color.) In any case, it was challenging enough to try to appear normal, but having such a boisterous and, well, famous father, didn't help much. I endured it as I always did, in a professional manner, by holding my cheeks in my hands to try to hide my embarrassment and fanning myself since I get rather sweaty when I feel nervous. See? Professional.

"Noblemen and noblewomen!" he started. Everyone sat up a little straighter when he started. He has that sort of effect on people. "My brother and I would like to welcome you to your apprenticeship. We decided to begin this program to introduce you all to your official duties. Each of you, have good faith and courage. Today, your lives begin. If you complete this process successfully, you will each become fully fledged members of our political society, and able to rule," he said that last part looking right at me. More redness. Everyone clapped politely, miraculously unaware of my blatant suffering.

Then my uncle began, beaming. "Yes! And while this is clearly not a competition, remember that those who perform exceptionally well will have the opportunity to serve in the king's court! I am expecting great things from all of you," he said, eyeing a girl who sat next to me in the front row. More polite claps.

"Then, my nobles, bring forth your best effort, and in three months time, we will have you ready for office!" With that, my father gathered his robes and exited, but of course not without his personal trumpet player denoting his exit.

"Now," Uncle Jacob added, "For this apprenticeship, you have each been given a region of our wonderful Promynthia to govern. But you will not go to your task alone! Each of you has been assigned a partner. As we reveal these, take some time amongst yourselves to walk around and speak to one another. As a country, we value unity above everything, so let us be united among our nobility!" Music began to play at that moment. In the other room, musicians began to serenade our ...meeting, I guess? The girl next to me turned to me now.

"Cousin!?" she exclaimed.

My eyes widened. "I— you...?"

"Yes, Arabella! I'm your cousin! My father is Prince Jacob Bysentor, that guy with the fancy pants robes over there," she clarified, pointing to him, as if I didn't know who she was talking about. She cocked her head to one side. "I guess your father doesn't speak of me much?" she paused. I blinked, not knowing what to say, and we passed an awkward moment in silence. "Never mind," she started again, rolling it off with a shrug of her shoulders, "It is nice to finally meet more family."

I nodded slowly, trying to process all the bubbly energy emitting from her. "And your name is?"

"Oh!" she exclaimed, giggling, putting a hand to her mouth as if catching some food that had fallen out. "I'm Crystal!" she grinned widely. Her yellow curls bounced freely atop her head in a big heap. Her pink gown was stunning, with tulle sheets and glittery stones atop thick, velvety fabric. To be honest, I was startled by how she seemed to be looking directly into my eyes, not through me like most when they saw my skin. She seemed surprisingly kind by the way her eyes sparkled and with her huge smiling face, but I didn't fully trust it. *What does she want?*

"So," she continued after my second awkward pause, "How do you feel about this whole apprenticeship thing?"

I sighed, chuckling a bit. I wasn't always the best with keeping up conversations when lost in thought. "Well, it will certainly be something, I guess."

"You've got that right!" she said, laughing and nudging my arm. I was shocked that she actually purposefully touched me. Most people keep their distance. Maybe she felt after all these years of silence from my uncle that she probably needed to form an alliance with me since I'd be ruling soon.

At this moment, a few other nobles stood near to us, some girls from the Wilian and Yori provinces. The Yori girl was laughing loudly with the Wilian one, and both seemed to have matching jet black hair. Crystal filled me in. "I met Tiffany and Elizabeth at the last Nobles' Banquet. Their provinces are pretty close to each other, and the people are related."

"I see," I said, eyeing them. I felt the sweat starting to form in my palms. Trying to shake it off, I asked Crystal, "Nobles' Banquet?"

Her wide grin dropped suddenly, and her mouth opened wide. "You don't know about the Banquet? We have it every year!"

"I'm sorry," I half-smiled looking down, "I don't really get out much, I guess."

"Oh, I'm sorry," she replied. "How often do you—" But before she could finish her next question, Willy and Yilly started walking in our direction.

"Hey guys!" Crystal called out to them. My heart started beating quickly, so I started tapping my foot lightly. Thank goodness this dress puffed out a lot— people usually couldn't tell if I was panicking or just plain dancing underneath...

Turning her head slowly, Elizabeth answered with a sly smile, "Crystal! It's been a while." She and Tiff sauntered over coolly, their elegance overwhelming me. Their long dresses featured off-shoulder, puffed sleeves, which seemed to only lengthen their long features. I felt small next to their graceful limbs.

"Yes, it really has!" Crystal nodded comfortably. "How are you both?"

"I've certainly been better," Tiffany said, and I am pretty sure that she stole a look at me at that moment, but maybe not. She cocked her head to one side now, fully facing me. "How does it feel to be practically a princess, Bella?" I stiffened at this casual greeting.

"Yes, and tell us your thoughts about the apprenticeship," Elizabeth added. It was funny. It's not like their words were impolite or outrageous. Yet, there was something about their very aura that screamed, *you don't belong here*. Maybe it was how they kept their attention focused on Crystal. Perhaps it was how they did the usual looking-through-me technique whenever they were forced to address me. This technique is when one Promynthian is trying to be "polite". Their words are technically politically correct, yet their body language says so much more. These subjects of mine judge me with their eyes, without even realizing they are doing it. Everything in their external actions is kind, yet their very essence communicates that I'm not really one of them.

Lucky for me, Uncle Jacob interrupted our little meeting. "Fellow nobles!" he began. "Commence to find your apprenticeship partner. You may begin your collaboration in our Grand Gardens." He motioned towards doors in the back of the room. Servants on either side opened them to reveal a magnificent pavilion wrapped in vines and itself surrounded by fields of greenery and an overabundance of flowers. It was absolutely breathtaking. And it reminded me of home.

As Uncle finished his instructions, I spun around from my lovely conversation, excitedly starting for the garden. Unfortunately, in my haste, I found myself spinning right into another noble.

Just my luck.

3

Boys

"Are you alright, Princess?"

"No, I am so sorry. I ran into you!" I shook my head violently, standing up quickly.

"It's quite alright," he said, pausing to look at me. "I'm Alexander," he said kindly. "What, um, what province are you in charge of?"

"Walabe, or specifically the Melindan island," I said, glancing at his hazel eyes nervously.

"That is excellent. You know, I am from there," he said. I looked at him with wide eyes. "I know! Most people don't know." He chuckled, and then began again. "I'm working on Clementia," he said, still smiling. His cheeks had deep dimples in them, which I caught myself staring at a little too long. At this point, we had made it to the pavilion, where everyone was finding their partners for the project.

"That is a beautiful province," I replied, smiling back. "My mother and I used to visit there often when I was a child and Father was out traveling."

"You mean you wouldn't go with your father?" I wanted to respond, but I was interrupted by a bubbly mess of curls.

"Hey!" Crystal said, excitedly curtsying.

"Hey, Crys, how have you been?" he asked her calmly, clearly used to the pomp and circumstance.

"Oh, just wonderful! It's so great to have you all here in the Dome with us. It gets kinda lonely with just me and Dad, and I need interaction!" she laughed aloud. I looked at her in amazement. I don't think I'd ever met someone with such joy bubbling over like that.

"How do you all even know each other?"

"The banquets," Alex replied shrugging. "And the annual balls too."

"I can't believe you haven't even been to one!" Crystal exclaimed. "They're probably my favorite part of the year," she added, closing her eyes, throwing her head back and beginning to sway back and forth. "What with the dresses, the dancing, the *romance*."

"Come back to us, Crys," Alex said, crossing his arms and rolling his eyes.

She burst into giggles again. "Sorry, guys," she answered, now twirling herself around with an imaginary partner. "I just get caught up in the moment, I guess," she added, flipping back her hair dramatically. At that moment, our conversation was broken up by a light tap on my shoulder, and I spun around again, attempting to be just as drama-filled as her and beginning to giggle, too.

"Princess?" a deep voice asked. My giggle got caught in my throat. I looked up... and up, and startling green eyes met my own. "My name is Augustus Theodore Frederick IX. I think we're partners for the Melindan island?"

I eyed my suddenly much less attractive friends desperately. "Oh," I managed to make out.

"Don't worry about them. They've got their own project," he said, chuckling. When I continued staring at him awkwardly, he tried motioning for us to walk ahead. Gingerly, I followed his gait heading in the direction of the lush fields. It was a bright day, so I quickly opened the umbrella I had with me.

"I can hold it for you," he offered, smiling now. "I hope you won't mind, it's just that I want our conversation to be private and away from the others so they don't steal our ideas!"

I laughed. "Haha, very true! And... thank you." Looking up at him from under my lace ceiling, at his lush brown wavy hair, I wondered what our partnership would look like.

"I'm from the Dome of Walabe," he started. "And where might you be from?" he added, daring to dash those dreamy eyes into my soul.

I giggled, trying to stop myself, but not being able to. "Well, of course I'm from the Capital. I was born and raised and haven't left since— well, until now."

"That's so interesting," he remarked, turning his gaze now to the lush fields we were now surrounded in. "How are you supposed to rule a world you haven't really seen?"

"I will," I replied quickly, "when the time is right. I am sure that the King and Queen know what they're doing."

He turned to me. "I'm sorry, I don't mean to point fingers," he added quietly. "I just want to make sure you're able to see *your* kingdom."

I nodded gratefully and nervously. "So, what do you want to do for this project?"

"We have to see what the city is like, to see if it is really as bad as they say."

"What have they come out with recently?" I was curious to hear his perspective.

"Melindans don't seem to embrace their... Promynthian roots. They kind of seem to be cutting themselves off from everyone else." I chuckled to myself. *Maybe it's the secluded island we've put them on?* I scoffed. August continued, "We've got to find a way to bring them in, you know?" I scrunched my nose at this. I'd heard this enough from Mother. I guess he noticed my change in expression. "What's wrong?"

"I don't know," I lied. "I guess, I just feel like, why are we trying to make them like us all the time? What's the point?" I thought about how much I wanted to just figure out who these people even were. Why did it feel like we were always trying to make everyone the same?

He nodded. "Well, what do you think we should do?"

I felt taken aback. It was wild that he actually wanted to hear my thoughts, since that didn't normally happen. I gave a half-smile. "Well, Idunno, maybe they separate themselves for a reason? Like, maybe they just think we don't like them or something."

He blinked a few times. "I wonder why they'd think that?" I thought about my conversations with Tiffany and Elizabeth and shuddered. I knew why. "Okay, well then, we can find a way to do that, to send them a message!" He smiled at me, pleased with our idea, and paused, looking at me wonderingly. "I do not think I have ever met a prettier Melindian."

"Oh, you are too kind!" I looked down, trying to hide my smile. I looked up at him again. I don't think anyone had gazed at me this way. I felt gripped with... nausea? No, I think those were butterflies in my stomach. Suddenly, this whole apprenticeship thing felt a little bit less impossible. Maybe, with Augustus's help, I wouldn't completely fail at this thing. Perhaps we could convince the Melindans that they are Promynthian at heart.

August and I continued our conversation for a while, until just before dinner. He was a pretty good listener, which I really appreciated. Finally, the dinner bell let us know we needed to head back inside.

"Oh, gosh, we've got to get dressed for the first dinner!" he said, placing a hand on my shoulder and chuckling. "Wow the clock went fast!" I smiled in agreement, before we ran back inside.

Back at the bedroom chamber, none other than Crystal was there to berate me with questions. "Arabella? How did it go?!" She asked, sitting on my bed, too excited to contain herself. I don't even know how she knew which bed was mine. I rolled my eyes at her, throwing off my dress to swap it for the dinner one. Hearing that she was trying to get information out of me, some other girls joined her around my bed.

"We saw you with August!" one girl called out.

"What did he say to you?" another chimed in.

"How tall is he again?" the third added.

I looked at them all, crowding around me. Honestly, I felt annoyed. None of these girls were trying to talk to me *before* I met my partner. Back when I was just the weird brown girl? Nothing. So, I just pursed my lips at them all and folded my arms. They got the message, and slowly sauntered away. Too bad, and I was just beginning to get popular. But, of course, Crystal stood her ground. She stood up quickly and pulled me into the hallway, her evening gown sweeping around her ankles. "Princess, you have to tell me!"

I rolled my eyes. "Calm down, Crys. Why does it even matter? We just talked about our jobs, isn't that what today was all about?"

"Sure," she replied, squinting her eyes. "That's what they *tell* you, but can't you see it? We've each been partnered to also test for our marriage potential. Don't you know they want us to meet that Future Someone out here?"

I blushed deeply, embarrassed for some reason about my initial interaction with August. Surely if there was any chance between us, my wild ideas probably had deterred him by now. "Wow," was about all I could get out.

She giggled, shaking her head at me. "You really are clueless, aren't you? Well, it doesn't matter. I think you've made quite the first impression on August!"

I raised an eyebrow. "You really think so?" I cleared my throat nervously, "Um, how do we know it was the right one?"

"Well, we don't, but we're going to find out. Tonight! At dinner," she stated, matter-of-factly. Linking her arm with mine, she began to stroll down the chamber hallway, of course dragging me with her. I just let her. "Arabella, why don't you think you have a chance with him?"

I looked at her. "Hey, Crys, I don't know what world you live in, but I am brown, which means.... I don't have a chance with *anybody*. I mean have *you* seen any inter-racial couples around here?"

She shook her head determinedly. "I've known August since we were kids, and I *know* when he's attracted to someone. You can trust me, he's never given me those vibes. Literally, my dad has *tried* putting us together.

"Uncle Jacob? " I asked. "Setting you two up?" By now, we were at the end of the hall, which opened up into the main hall. I looked up for a moment, noticing the dark starry sky above us through the glass dome.

"Of course!" she replied, rolling her eyes. "I mean, obviously it would be great since he loves his dad. I mean, literally, the Duke of Walabe is basically royalty. August is as close to a prince as you're going to get in our "great nation."

I paused, looking at her. "You really don't seem that hung up over this."

"Sweetheart," she began, rolling her eyes. "I don't like these Promynthian boys." She had my full attention now. Giggling, she added with a whisper, "I'd much rather marry a Melindan!"

I looked at her, wide eyed with wonder. This girl had quite the personality. Naturally, I burst out laughing and she joined me. Before anyone could notice our foolishness, we made our way back down the hall to our chambers. I'm pretty sure I found my new friend in this place.

Once we were dressed and ready to eat, we headed to gather in the evening chamber for dinner. From within the gray stone-walled room, a gorgeous smell of warm roasted chicken beckoned me closer and closer in. I closed my eyes for a moment, just to take in the aroma. As I peered in shyly, I realized that the whole room was extremely cozy. Besides the gigantic wooden table in the middle that stretched across much of the room, there was a blazing fireplace, soft area rugs made of various fluffy materials, thick chairs surrounding the fireplace for more lounging and a backdrop of countless books that decorated the somewhat aged, stone walls.

Interrupting my thoughts, Crystal came up from behind me and nudged me with her elbow, flashing a bright smile. "Are you ready?" She motioned for us to link arms again, to which I agreed happily. Together we marched in and then sat next to each other. I was amazed at how quickly I was beginning to bond with my cousin. She was just so inviting and kind and warm. Glancing over the table, I spotted my cinnamon tea. But as I began to reach across the long table for it, I suddenly stopped as my uncle began making an announcement.

"Greetings, Nobles and welcome to your first dinner!" he started. After his speech concerning rules about staying in your own chamber, curfew for the night, not stealing and such, I began tuning out and thinking of the cinnamon tea. I imagined its spicy flavor in my mouth and couldn't resist but reach out for it. Unfortunately, my arm was just a lot shorter than I was expecting and I was unable to fully reach it, even though I really stretched myself out pretty far. Then I locked eyes with a tall someone who was willing to help from across the table and was now currently holding a cinnamon tea bag in hand. August.

"Princess!" my uncle snapped. Startled, I jumped in my seat. Of course, people started to giggle quietly. I felt my face beginning to get hot. "Would you be so kind as to pay attention to the rules of our apprenticeship?"

That's when August spoke up in my defense, to my great surprise, to be honest. Passing me the cinnamon bag gently, he addressed my uncle as if they were old friends. "Jacob, I completely understand your frustration, but do see that the princess here was merely awaiting a sip of tea, and was not brought one by our staff. It was all she could do to quietly get it herself without disrupting anyone!" My uncle narrowed his eyes and paused for a moment.

"Very well then," he replied. I shot a look back at August, who was now sitting and steadily eyeing me. Then he *winked* at me. I think I almost fell over inside.

"Did you get your tea?" Crystal whispered to me as Uncle Jacob continued on. It took me a minute to process her question. I was so stunned by what had just occurred.

"...what? Oh, yes!" I whispered back, carefully peeling back the delicate papers to reveal its delicious cinnamon contents! Looking over my shoulder again, I caught August still staring. I turned back around quickly. "Oh gosh, he's still looking at us!"

"Not us, dear. *You!* " she whispered back quickly. I felt faint. Why was this happening to me? At the end of the speech, the musicians began to play and we all were able to start eating away at our food. They had decorated the chamber beautifully, probably to welcome us to our new home. The tables themselves had sweeping tablecloths, while thick burgundy curtains hung on the walls. A roaring fire crackled away in the fireplace, but that could hardly be heard among the lively nobles chittering away between small talk and all the latest district news.

For dinner we enjoyed rosemary roasted chicken with peppered baked potatoes and some greenery. I wanted to give the chefs a pay raise when I tasted that food. But then again, maybe I was just extra hungry! For dessert, we enjoyed decadent brownies with hot chocolate syrup. Between that and the many cups of tea, I was having quite the evening. As I neared the end of my third brownie, Crystal gave me a hard nudge with her elbow. "Ow! What was that for—"

"Excuse me," a deep voice said. Startled, I looked to my left and of course it was him again.

"Oh, hey, August," I managed to say casually. He smiled.

"Can I speak with you outside?"

"Well, sure," I heard myself reply. In a moment, there we were, standing side by side on the pavilion, looking out over the now dark fields. The stark moonlight contrasted starkly against the deep night sky while sparking dust glittered across the rest of the expanse. I took a deep breath.

"How was dinner?" he asked me.

Oh gosh, small talk. What was this about? "I'm good," I replied, shrugging. "Um, how about you?"

"It was great" he said.

"Well, thanks for the tea," I added.

"Oh sure! Yeah, Bysentor is just cranky sometimes, he'll smooth over," he replied, chuckling.

"I guess you know him then?"

"Yeah, he's cool. He and my dad are close, I guess." Then looking at me, he added, "I don't really know how to say this, but I'm really looking forward to working with you on this project, Arabella." My breaths became shallower. I stood there, frozen and unsure of what to say.

"I..." I managed to get out.

"You know, you're cute when you don't know what to say."

"I..."

"Say you'll give me a chance to prove myself to you," he said, reaching for my hands now. My eyes widened, looking at my own hands held between his, completely stunned. Dumbfounded, I looked back at him.

"Um," I said, blushing now. "Yes, I will," I managed to get out. He flashed a grin at me, and squeezed my hands tight.

"Great," he replied, and then, plucking a lily from the nearby bush, he placed it in my hair and then hurried back inside. So there I sat, all blushing and shocked and considerably happy. Which is right when Crystal appeared from behind who knows where squealing.

"Eeeeee!" she said.

"Gah! How did you get out here?" I asked, startled.

"I've been following you the whole time," she admitted. When I gave her a look of annoyance, she added, "What?"

"Can't you give me any privacy, woman?"

Giggling, she ignored me. I shook my head. This was a wild one indeed. "So... I've been thinking about you and how you're here in Cyrote now, and well, was wondering if you wanted to see Melinda for yourself?" I scrunched my eyebrows in confusion for a moment, which is when another figure appeared from the bushes.

"Alex!" I said, startled. Turning to both of them I added, "Hey, can you guys stop just popping up all over? I don't think I can handle it," I said, chuckling.

"Yeah, sorry about her, she's a *live* one." Alex said, shaking his head. "Anyway, Crys also knows that I know the island pretty well, so she wants me to show it to you."

"...and you think this might help me with my project?" I questioned, looking from him to Crystal.

Without waiting for my response, she exclaimed. "She's in!"

At this, I quickly held up my hands. "Listen, y'all. You might be fine just doing whatever, but I'm, like, royalty, and I need to make sure I do this thing right so..." I trailed off, shrugging my shoulders and feeling like a bit of a loser, "I guess I'm out?"

Crystal's shoulders sank. "But!"

"No, Crystal, I'm sorry but I'm headed back inside," I replied, shaking my head and turning away. I couldn't let anything get me off track from what I came here to do— get my coronation.

4

Monday

I got up before the sun the next morning. Nerves always messed with my sleep, either making me crazy tired or not really tired at all. I didn't really get much rest that night anyway. I shook my head as I pulled off my covers. *What if Crystal and Alex were right and I should meet other Melindans? Did I just burn some bridges or something?* I pursed my lips. They would just have to wait, because I didn't know the first thing about ruling a country, let alone a city. And, isn't that what this whole apprenticeship was for anyway?

Trying to distract myself from the guilt of not going with them, I spent an extra-long time in the shower. At least it smelled all good in there, what with the sea scented soap they had for us there. It was not as luxurious at my strawberry scents at home, but what's a girl to do in her uncle's palace?

Feeling more refreshed, I headed to the breakfast chamber, hoping I could slip in and out before the others. But unfortunately, one other had the same idea. Yeah, you guessed it, it was August. He looked up at me from the long rectangular table they had set up, either surprised or happy to see me. *Was he hoping to catch me here?* "Arabella!" he began, shooting those green eyes at me. I tried to hide my grin, though not with much success.

"Hey," I managed to get out, but for some reason, I was too starstruck to even move. He rescued the moment though, with a chuckle.

"Are you, uh, going to get some food?" he suggested, tilting his head slowly to the meal table, which was filled with decadent, flaked pastries, hard-boiled eggs, coffee, biscuits and thinly sliced fruit piled in glass dishes.

Suddenly, I wasn't so hungry though. "Oh," I replied weakly, realizing that I was so debilitated that I couldn't even manage to function properly. *Stupid! He's going to think you're a weirdo who doesn't eat breakfast or something. Say something!* But it was really all I could do not to just fall over or run out of the room from embarrassment. Thankfully, the rest of the nobles started trickling in, coming to my rescue and saving me from this moment. I guess August realized I needed saving too, because he had just finished eating and was now walking over to me. *Stop staring, Arabella! Look natural.* So I did the most natural thing I could, and started pulling at the elbow part of my sleeve, while looking down to adjust... who knows what... with my shoe.

That's when a perfectly tailored, brown oxford shoe and khaki pants entered my visual frame. "Want some tea?" August asked, interrupting my very important and deliberate task of shoe fiddling, and now standing dangerously close to me.

I looked up at him slowly, cheeks now blazing. "Sure," I

breathed, wiping some hair away that wasn't even in my face. I watched as his perfect cheeks widened into a grin, before he turned on his heels to get me something to drink.

Returning a few moments later, he added, "Want to get outside? It's a beautiful morning and I know you like those flowers and all."

I looked back at the other nobles getting louder as they started reminiscing on something they must have all experienced. I guess more annual ball members reuniting. I turned back to my handsome ticket out of there and smiled. "Sure."

The sun was shining radiantly that morning, and I definitely appreciated being away from the now loud breakfast chamber. Maybe I wasn't so great with people like I thought I was. Or maybe it was just hard to connect with a conglomerate who collectively thought you were a weird color. I nestled into the bench I was sitting at, and tried to feel comfortable, even though I was more than nervous to be sitting just a few inches from August. He turned to me now, swinging his knees in my direction and placing an arm on the back of the bench. "So," he started, "tell me about yourself."

I took a sip of tea, pleased that it was cinnamon. "You remembered!"

"Naturally," he shrugged.

I smiled. "What is it you want to know?" I asked, tossing some of my curls back.

"First, what's it like being a princess?"

I rolled my eyes. "Stressful." His face fell quickly, so I laughed. "What? Not what you expected?"

"Not at all," he chuckled back.

"Well, that's just it," I added, scrunching my shoulders for some reason. "I'm just an unpredictable person, that's all."

"Yes, you are," he replied, letting his hand inch a little closer to my shoulder, which was also conveniently resting on the back of the bench. Clearing his throat, he continued, "I guess I just thought it would be fun, you know, having all that power and everything."

"Fun?" I exclaimed. "This isn't some fantasy world, August. All that power means that people will have to listen to me, which means I need to actually know what I'm talking about."

"I guess that's fair."

"Plus," I added, feeling frustration welling up, "I don't know the first *thing* about weilding power like that. I mean, it's not like people really listen to girls anyway. Or Melindans. And, um, I'm both..."

"I'm listening to you right now," he countered.

"But that's because you think I'm pretty—" I started but then clapped my hands over my mouth, hiding some of the flushing coming to my cheeks. *Not the right words, Bella, not the right words at all.*

But luckily, August didn't seem to mind. Instead, he bent doubled over, and slapped his thigh emphatically while getting into a laughing spell. I guess it was sort of funny. I started giggling too. Finally, he sat up. "Well, you're right about one thing, Arabella. You definitely are pretty. But that's not the only reason I'm listening to you."

I was intrigued now. "Well then, why else?"

He half-smiled in response. "I guess you're just going to have to find out," he winked.

For the first time, I smiled directly into his eyes, letting my heart sit in them for a moment. "I intend to."

5

Friday

Liking a boy is somehow so much more intriguing when you're in their presence. That's how it felt being around Sir Augustus Frederick IX. I think there's something utterly intoxicating about it. I felt equally giddy and panic-stricken at the same time. *Does he like me? Does he think my hair is cute? How's my dress?* Some would call this insecurity. I like to call it doing my best to be attractive to him. Because, it's just like my mom said, I could find the next king of Promynthia here. I smiled to myself. *Maybe I've already found him.*

Before I could talk myself out of my next move, I walked determinedly to the seat right next to him in the front of the room, ready for City Ruling 101. Several eyes followed me to that seat, smack dab in the front middle of the room. I tried to ignore the fact that I felt like a peanut floating in a sea of buttermilk and instead focused on those endlessly green eyes.

"Hey Arabella," he said, flashing a sweet smile my way.

"Hey," I replied quietly, looking up and him first and then

at the front to see if our professor was going to start speaking. And not a moment too soon.

"Good morning, Nobles. My name is Professor Winston, and I will be your apprenticeship master for the duration of the summer. Also, since this is currently the pilot of this program, I am learning as much as you, so I will appreciate your great patience!" A gentle chuckle spread throughout the room. I nodded, trying to show that I was engaged and listening.

As he went on to describe how this program was created and how important it was, I did let my mind drift however to question some things. Like, *why was his beard so long?* It was wiry and straight and full, without much direction or intention. It seemed like it was not really part of his face. Also, there wasn't a single streak of gray in it. Actually, I blinked a few times to make sure I was seeing correctly. He was actually much younger than I had imagined. He was, maybe, 25 at the most? I was shocked that they allowed someone so young around here. I think the beard aged him though. *Definitely not a great look.* However, he did have these earnest brown eyes. They were just so comforting, like he was really seeing me, even right now, and not through me—

"Will you, Arabella?"

"Wait, what?" I replied, shocked out of my thoughts.

"Will you introduce yourself to the class?" Professor Winston asked again.

"Oh yes, of course!" I said quickly, shooting out of my seat and turning around. And that's when the clammy hands started, because I actually had to address these people. And I don't think I made the best impression with accidentally trailing off in my thoughts. But, the show had to continue. "Hey, um, I'm Arabella," I started, with a slight wave. Some chuckles went across the room. "Um, right, you already know that. Yeah, so anyway, I am from the Grand Palace." More giggles. Heat filled my cheeks. This needed to go faster. "So yeah, obviously I'm here to learn how to rule you all—" Uproarious laughter now filled the room. "I mean—" I tried over the shouts of glee and flung back heads. "I mean to rule the kingdom!" But it was of no use. I'd lost them and I'd never even had them. This was too much. Before causing any more damage, I pulled up the bottom of my skirt and rushed out of the room.

In the hallway, my face felt a little less tight and hot. I inhaled deeply. At least I could breathe out here. I shook my head. *They didn't take me seriously for one minute*, I thought, shaking my head in shame. I sat there on the floor for the remainder of the 50 minutes we were in session. I mean, what was I supposed to do? If I went back to my bedroom chamber, I might run into Uncle Jacob or a guard and get in trouble for not being in class. And if I went back into class... well that was clearly not an option. Instead I made myself comfortable on the floor. At least my skirt was so nice and fluffy that it felt like a whole blanket.

Eventually, class let out and the other nobles filed out noisily. Most didn't even look down to see or notice me. I was glad of it. I think I wanted to disappear right then anyway. Once things seemed quiet, I stood up quietly to head back to my room. But I guess I stood a moment too soon, because there were still two students in there with Professor Winston.

"Arabella, are you all right?" Professor Winston asked me earnestly. He, Crystal and Alexander were all walking out of the room at that moment, I guess in some deep conversation or something. For a moment I was speechless. *He actually cares?*

"Um, yes I'm okay."

"Good, good," he said, seeming relieved. "I'm sorry about all the laughing in there. I wasn't trying to embarrass anyone."

"I know," I replied, shrugging my shoulders. But then I looked back up. He was still looking at me earnestly, pausing to see if he could see past my answer. It was like he really cared about me in the same way he cared for those other nobles, or maybe, like he cared more.

"You know, Arabella, since you are focusing on the Melindans for your project, it could be helpful to actually visit their island." I stood there for a moment feeling uncomfortable. *Did Alexander really bring this up to our new professor?*

Now it was Alexander who spoke up. "Princess, you really should see your own people for yourself." I didn't really know what to say. I mean, a professor was standing right there. What if we got in trouble?

"I won't say anything!" Professor Winston replied with his palms in the air, almost as if reading my thoughts. "But I will say," he added, readjusting his golden rims, "that this would be quite the opportunity for you to understand the nature of your country. I highly endorse all of my students to understand their assigned territory, but especially the next ruler of our country."

I was shocked. He seemed to be really invested in me ruling. I guess that was a good thing, since it was up to him to decide if I passed or failed this whole thing anyway.

"Thanks for the suggestion," I said, smiling a little. And then, something clicked. *What was I being so afraid of anyway?*It seemed even my professor wanted me to go. I decided to let go of whatever was holding me back. "I *guess* we could go then," I added, shrugging.

"Oooo!" Crystal squealed. "When do we go, when do we go?!"

Alexander grinned at me and her, as if he was eagerly awaiting this moment. "Tonight."

6

Village

As dusk fell upon the city, Alexander and I mounted atop horses to make our way towards the island. We disguised ourselves with sweeping brown cloaks so we wouldn't be recognized by any locals, or at least not by the provincial guards we needed to sneak past. Under my cloak, I wore dark leather pants in place of my usual gown. I also had laced-up boots and a cotton white long-sleeved blouse. Alexander was similarly dressed, but he looked much more natural and in his element than I. We were about to leave, when a blond haired ghost came out of the darkness to meet us. I screamed, "Ahhh!"

"Arabella, it's me!" Crystal said, holding up her arms. "Shut up, silly, or the guards will hear you," she whispered, giggling to herself. In a flash she had mounted a beautiful grey horse and was ready to join us. She too wore a brown cloak, and she also sported white leather pants and a brown blouse. I just looked at her, happily grinning at me and Alexander.

"I was about to ask where you were," Alexander said,

rolling his eyes like this was the most normal interaction in the world. With the three of us ready to go, we headed out.

"It's a beautiful night, Princess!" he said, once we had made it about a quarter mile down the road.

"I agree," I smiled, gazing at the sky. It was big and black and beautiful, with little pin pricks of light shining through. I was probably imagining it, but I almost felt like the stars were calling out to me somehow, like the light beckoned me in from somehwere. As we got a better view of the island once we had traveled for a bit, I noticed a pattern of lights high up on top of the mountain, all clustered together. "Why do the people live so high up on the island?" I asked him.

"There's only paths that lead up to the top. I've only seen Promynthian vacationists spending time on the bottom," he replied, chuckling. "It's way too hot down there, and the locals know the cool breeze that reaches them from the water is much better." He shook his head. "Not everything the Promynthians do is right, you know."

"Well, of course not," I said annoyed, rolling my eyes. But internally, I sort of chuckled too. It was funny to imagine rich nobles being scorched at the bottom of the mountain as they thought they were in some sort of paradise. These Melindansseemed pretty smart and I liked that.

Finally, we made it to the island entrance, which was a narrow dock over the vast body of water. I won't lie and say I wasn't a little nervous that my horsy-horse would trip over the narrow dock and land us in the water. But, he didn't miss one step. After we crossed, we made our way up the steep mountain paths. I appreciated the strength of my steed, who just steadily trotted uphill. In a kind gesture, I smoothed his mane, whispering, "You're doing so great," to hopefully encourage him. Finally, we made it to the top, where the village was awake and alive.

Flashes of color from vibrant tapestries and a steady glowing of fires in the buildings high up above met my eyes. The shops, decorated outside by hanging lanterns and intricate fabrics, were made of sturdy wooden beams thatched together with natural vines. Accents included stone facing, no doubt from the rocky paths we had just passed on our way here. Most strikingly, in place of the familiar silence of most Promynthian provinces, a steady hum of village life surrounded the place.

Jumping down from his horse and tying him to a tree, Alexander looked up at me. "Need a hand?" I looked over at Crystal, who had already dismounted and was now carefully pulling out a rope for her own ride.

"No, I've got it," I replied. *If she can do it, can't I?* I paused looking at the ground. "Well, actually," I said again, thinking of how I had been banned from horseback lessons from my way too overprotective parents.

"No worries, Princess," he said with his hands in the air, coming over to assist me.

"You know, you can call me Arabella, Alexander." I said, squinting at him in annoyance, even as he helped me down from my horse.

"Oh, right, yeah!" he replied, seeming a bit nervous for some reason. "I guess then you should call me Alex!" he said with a smirk, tying my horse as well. Then, he looked at me for a moment, thinking, and then added with a nod, "You know, you should take your hair down. It'll help you blend in more." He raised his eyebrows at my neat bun, complete with an elaborate string of pearls and a few flowers.

"Oh," I said, looking up and feeling suddenly self-conscious. A few minutes later, I had loosened my braids to unleash my unruly curls. I paused, closing my eyes and smiling, reflecting on this moment. It actually felt good to be free.

"Ready?" he asked me. Linking arms together, we entered the nearest, loudest tavern.

Once inside, I observed my surroundings. The place was made completely of oak, similar to the rest of the village buildings. It had an organic smell to it, very earthy really. And there was an irresistible smell coming from the back room, which I could only assume must be the kitchen. I smiled warmly at my new friends. "Thank you for bringing me here," I said. They nodded happily. We waited for a minute and then were seated at a nearby booth on the left wall of the restaurant. I breathed in deeply. Something warm and spicy was cooking up in that kitchen and I needed to taste it.

Suddenly, a young woman, who couldn't have been older than me, appeared at our table with a grin. As Alex ordered, I stared at her and probably too long not to be noticed. I was honestly startled by her appearance. A darker or smoother complexion had never met my eyes before. My own skin was speckled with tiny freckles and moles from one too many times outside without my umbrella, but the sun seemed only to enhance her natural beauty. And her hair- was it twisted or knotted, perhaps? Somehow, it was fashioned into thick, strong chords that danced around her waist. Golden bands wrapped around these strands, complementing her beautiful, ebony shaded eyes.

"And what can I get for you, Missy?" she asked me, flashing a white smile my way that contrasted her deep color. My cheeks reddened as I glanced down at the strange menu with words I'd never seen before, wondering if perhaps they had cinnamon tea. I had never ordered at a tavern before.

"I— um, I'll just get whatever Alex is having," I replied, motioning towards him. Hopefully he knew what to get. A wave of sadness passed over me. I realized that here I was, in the heart of the Melindans, and had absolutely no idea what these foods even were.

"Perfect!" she said, winking at Alex and then quickly spinning around again to head to the kitchen. Her long chords of hair following in a twirl. I watched her slink gracefully to the kitchen wondering who she was.

"Wow, you really can't hide what you're feeling inside, can you?" Crystal asked me, interrupting my brooding thoughts. "I mean, it's amazing! I really feel like I'm reading your mind or something." She laughed.

"I'm sorry," I said nervously, "I've just never seen..."

"A real Melindan up close. I know," Alex added, nodding.

"They're so... beautiful," I said, both surprised by the truth of that and also by the pang of sadness that Alex brought up. *Aren't I a real Melindan too?* But there was no time for that in the midst of conversation. Crystal was nodding in agreement with Alex.

"Yeah, these people are definitely nothing like Father describes," she commented. I raised an eyebrow at her.

"What do you mean?" I asked. "What does he say about them?" Even Alex leaned forward intently to listen.

"Well," she said, rolling her eyes away from us and sighing

deeply, "he certainly doesn't *like* them, if that's what you're wondering. He's always talking about how they're angry and rude and lazy and basically anything negative you can think of. As a kid, I definitely wasn't allowed to play with anyone who looked even remotely Melindan, lest I get any ideas to be like them, of course."

I smirked at her. "And what's wrong with them?" I asked, crossing my arms.

"Nothing!" she exclaimed, shaking her head fervently. "I don't actually agree with my father, you know."

"You know, it's interesting," I began, after pausing a moment. "I wasn't allowed to play with anyone who looked Melindan either."

Alex chuckled. "*That's* something there, Arabella."

"I know!" I said, looking at him. "I mean, seriously I would sometimes see servants and think to myself how lucky I was not to look like them. Although I do really appreciate Julian, because he's so kind to me always." I sighed. "It's like my entire life I've just been set up to see people in a certain way, just because of how they look."

Crystal nodded her head. "I feel the same way," she added. "Except, I always had the luxury to choose not to listen to those silly things, because of course they were obviously false. Usually, I'd just roll my eyes at whoever was saying the nonsense and continue on my way."

I stopped to ponder her comment. She was right. It was impossible for me to think the same way as her. I sat there for a moment, just thinking of all the times I had tried pushing these thoughts away, telling myself they weren't real— that I wasn't a monster that needed to hide away. It would probably have been different had I been able to just forget about the whole thing. But my mirror faithfully reminded me each day of my plight, of the plight of my people. I closed my eyes for a moment. "How could we—"

"Treat people the way we do? Hide them away? Dehumanize them?" He raised an eyebrow, shrugging now. "Welcome to the Promynthian Way, Princess."

The Promynthian Way. I could almost hear my father talking about it in the courts, when I would be sitting in the back room listening in on his rulings and speeches to the people or to the nobles. It was an ideal that our country held dear, that our way of life would be the solution to the world. This gave us the right to take other lands as we wanted, to correct them, if you will, to help the "helpless."

As if reading my mind, Alex interrupted my thoughts. "Arabella, do you really think these people need help?" I observed the room again, wanting a fresh look. The tavern was a humbly fashioned building, but the people within it were certainly far from destitute. In fact, far from this, they were full of life. Couples entertained one another with stories and threw their heads back in uncontrollable laughter. Skilled musicians played their craft in the tavern's corner, serenading not only their audience but the entire village. Brown bodies danced together on the dirt floor, spinning, twisting, and smiling. It was beautiful.

I turned back toward Alex, who was humming along contentedly to the music. "And, how do you know of this place?" Crystal and I waited in anticipation for his response.

He sighed. "My parents never agreed with Promynthia's values of 'unity.' They always wanted to teach me the views of all of our people, including the conquered ones." He smiled, reminiscing of their memories. "They said the best leaders truly know all of their people, and they especially loved the Melindans. They chose to raise me here in their honor."

"And... where are your parents now?" I asked, confused. But Alex's attention shifted immediately to a white, hooded figure that passed by us and sat a few tables away from us. That's when the expression on Alex's face grew extremely dim. He grabbed my hand and said in a low voice, "We have to leave. Now!"

"Wait, why?" But before I could demand an answer from him or question why he grabbed my hand and not Crystal's, our waitress was back at our table with a blank check.

"I guess it's a short stay tonight, Alex!" she said, quickly. "I've got your horses around the back. Go to the usual exit through the kitchen." Quickly, she spun around again with a wide smile to wait on the hooded figure.

"Now's our chance!" he whispered to us. Still holding me, he pulled me so that we made our way towards the kitchen. Crystal followed close behind. Just as we were about to exit, two surly men stood in our paths, grimacing. I froze with fear but Alex quickly pushed me straight to the ground so I could slip through their legs. Crystal was quickly down after me.

As I fell down, I looked back to see the silver flashing of two long knives appearing from deep within his cloak. They quickly sank into the flesh of the surly men's arms. Amidst their screams of pain, he dove to the ground after me and dragged me out of the kitchen. Behind us, the men scrambled after us. Alex pulled back the curtain that served for the back door to reveal our two horses. Frantically, he pushed me onto my horse and then swung his leg up and around his own. Crystal had somehow already mounted. The three of us rounded the back and were deep in the woods before the injured men could catch up to us.

Back at the safety of the Dome, we stealthily returned our horses to their stables.

"We'll have to climb the Dome wall to the windows so we aren't seen by the palace guards at the front entrance," he whispered, pointing to the stone walls. "Otherwise, they'll report us to the prince... and that won't be great for our heads or this apprenticeship!"

"How often do you sneak out at night anyway?" Crystal hissed, furrowing her brows. He didn't answer, but motioned for me to be quiet, as a guard patrolled nearby. Next, he ran ahead, crouching low to the ground and beckoning for us to follow. A minute later we had reached the wall. We climbed a tree growing adjacent to the palace and he hopped inside. Then, he assisted us as we jumped in from the tree, one after the other. We were safely inside now, but had landed right into the dank dungeon corridors. It wasn't more than a big dark cave with holes carved out for sunlight. Clearly, no one had dusted for years probably, judging by the cobwebs all over the ceiling. The air smelled musty and thick, and the only lights were the lanterns burning away hung across the walls of the place. We took a moment to catch our breath, and then we berated Alex with questions.

"So, what just happened?" Crystal began.

"Those— those are the Watchers," he replied, catching his breath still.

"What! What are the 'Watchers?' And why did you bring me out there if you knew they were there?" I chimed in.

"Not everyone is on your side, Princess."

"Excuse me?" I asked, raising my voice a little.

"I'm just saying, don't take offense!" he defended himself. "Listen, the Watchers are a group that believes that Promynthians should only be... a certain way. They make sure that no one else, especially the Melindans, have access to their power. They recognized you in the village and were just... trying to get rid of me to get to you. We'll just have to go back tomorrow to let you meet more people." My eyes widened.

"What are you talking about Alex?" Crystal asked frantically.

"Get to me?" I asked, stunned. "Why would they—"

But I was interrupted by Alex covering my mouth with his sweaty palm. Deftly, he pulled me back into a dark corner of the dungeon. Crystal had already jumped back, being the first to notice. That's when I saw the flickering light that had sprung him into action.

"Hello?" a deep voice called out. The voice got closer, and then was joined by a tall body. It was August, holding a candle.

"I'll explain tomorrow on the road," Alex said, hardly audibly. "Let's meet at the stable after breakfast." I looked back at him, confused, but he suddenly pushed me out of the corner, with himself and Crystal still hidden. I stumbled out.

"Show yourself!" August shouted aggressively, drawing his shiny sword to meet my startled, now wide eyes. I stood very still.

"Arabella?" he asked, blinking and startled. He slowly lowered his weapon. "What are you doing in the dungeon corridors at this time of night? If your uncle saw us speaking right now—" But I cut him off.

"August!" I quickly hugged him, shaking and finally safe from the chasing of the night.

"Okay, okay," he said, looking down at me and chuckling as he wrapped me in his arms. "Are you sure you're alright?" he asked, confusion spreading across his face as he surveyed my cloak, pants and free hair.

"I just went out for an evening stroll and lost track of the time," I lied. "So, I climbed up a tree so I wouldn't get caught... and, here I am?"

"Well," he said warmly, not letting go of me, "as long as you're okay. Goodness, I could have hurt you!" I held onto his well-built arm and rested my head contentedly on his broad, secure shoulder, smiling. *You could never hurt me August,* I thought contentedly to myself. Together, we strolled out of the dungeon and he guided me back to my sleeping chambers, before sweetly wishing me goodnight.

7

Breakfast

Soft, free-flowing music washed over me. Sounds of laughter filled my ears and the mouths of those around me. I smiled, styling a white lily behind my left ear and brushing back my hair. She was so happy, sitting there, her plump round figure softly brushing against my own as we sat close. Her brown hands skillfully plucked at the strings of her mandolin as she crooned out a beautiful lullaby:

Qua ye ye tutini, Mana
You are one of a kind, my darling
Shoni tu faya qua yeye li
And safe and warm you will stay
Fi yaye Wi Shi tufeni qua
Our Creator, He loves you so
Sho qua tokeni parsel.
And you must know today.

Gratefully, I hugged her in response as she continued. "Won't you teach me too, Nani?" Her warm, brown eyes met my own, beaming.

"Wake up, Arabella," she said, softly. "Wake up!"

"Wake up, silly!" Crystal whispered to me, nudging me aggressively. She had snuck into my chamber that morning and was currently hovering over my basically lifeless body. I rolled over to meet her wide eyes. "Wha...?" I began. But she ignored my sleepy confusion.

"Bella, we've got to talk," With that, she tiptoed out of my room, barefoot, of course with her white nightgown trailing angelically behind her, and motioned for me to follow her. I rolled my eyes, but smiled a little too. She was so crazy sometimes. Shaking my head, I forced myself from my sheets and followed her down the cold hallway.

In a few minutes, we were sitting outside at the familiar garden gazebo. It was dawn, and the sun was just beginning to rise now, painting the pale blue sky in tints of salmon and gold. Sitting on a bench, she motioned for me to join her. I did, curling up my knees and hugging them close to my chest, feeling comfy on the little bench. "What's going on, Crys?" I asked.

"No, it's not about me. I'm worried about you!" she exclaimed. "Are you okay from yesterday? That was sort of... a lot. And how did things go with August last night?"

I giggled. Not because I thought they were funny questions, but because sometimes I laugh when I'm nervous. "Come on," she continued, "I need to know— did he suspect anything? You're not going to tell your parents, are you?"

"No. Thankfully, he was just happy I was okay," I sighed, slowly letting out the stress I was bottling up inside. I could tell she was relieved too. I guess she didn't exactly want her father, Mr. Prince, knowing what she was up to either. I continued, "But I'd never tell my parents, you know." She looked a little surprised, so I explained further, "I'm just getting started learning about my people. How could I stop that now? Besides, my parents would just be worried about me and want me home."

She nodded. "That makes sense. Sorry to hear that they're sort of... protective, I guess." She paused, a worried look spreading across her face again. "Although that is sort of understandable considering last night." She eyed me again. I nodded in agreement.

"But, Crys, they can't keep me hidden forever, and that's the problem. I've never so much as seen someone who looks like me until now. I can't take my own chance away."

"That's true," she agreed. "And August, he didn't think it was strange to see you in the dungeon in the middle of the night?"

"Nope!" I grinned. "He *trusts* me, Crys. And someday, I'm going to bring him to the Melindans too." I didn't tell her how I thought it was honestly strange that *he* was in the dungeon last night.

"Nice," she replied, finally sure that our tracks were decently covered. Feeling more relaxed, she looked out over the multicolored horizon, taking in the scenery. A high pitched symphony of morning birds could be heard in the surrounding trees. A cool morning breeze greeted us and the flowers in the garden. A faint smell of breakfast was rising from the smokestacks at the Dome behind us. My stomach began to grumble in response. Oblivious, Crystal continued, "He's really nice to you, isn't he?"

Then I forgot my stomach. "He's kind of dreamy, really," I

blushed. "So gentle and kind. He's always checking to make sure I'm okay."

"That's so great, Bella," she replied. Then she touched my shoulder and looked very serious now. "And it had better stay that way."

I was shocked. "Crys?"

"What? If he were to so much as lift a finger wrongly in your direction, I would personally murder him!"

I blinked at her incredulously, eyeing her fists clenching tightly now and her face hardening under her innocent curls. "Those are some incredible fighting words, my friend!"

"What do you expect?" she asked, shrugging. "I *am* your personal body guard. That's the job of every best friend." We paused and then both broke out laughing before heading inside to change and get ready for the day. But on the way back inside, I did let one more question out under my breath.

"You don't think Professor Winston was behind any of that, do you?"

"No. Why?"

I shrugged. "I guess he just seemed so invested in us going. What if he wanted me to get hurt?"

She shook her head vehemently. "No, he's literally the sweetest. I think he just really cares about you, that's all. He wants you to know your people." She giggled. "Plus, he's a professor. How could a teacher be behind some sort of violent operation like that?" I thought about that for a moment. He was really nice. Maybe he was just looking out for me? And besides, he was just a nerdy professor. In any case, I looked forward to getting more questions answered by Alex.

But for some reason, at breakfast, he barely even looked

in my direction. It was as if nothing had even happened the night before. I scrunched my eyebrows at him from across the breakfast table, confused.

"Hey, Bella? You okay?" August asked, nudging me with his elbow. I had decided to make a practice of sitting with him.

"What?" I turned to him. "Oh, yeah, I'm fine. I just have a lot on my mind."

"Oh okay," he said, but then his face turned to panic. "Since last night, you mean? You're not thinking of quitting the apprenticeship, are you?"

"August," I said, surprised. "What are you talking about? I just wanted to take a nice stroll, not run away. Even princesses like the night sky, you know."

"I know," he said with a half-smile. "I guess, well... I just got worried about you, that's all. You just seemed quiet today and I would never want you to feel unsafe with me, especially after I accidentally pointed a sword in your face."

"Hey, if anything, you just wanted to protect me. Plus, I care about my kingdom. Besides, I have my reasons to stay."

He smiled at me again. "I know," he said, holding my hand now. "Hey, when are we going to talk about the project?"

"How about tomorrow?"

"It's a date, then." He winked at me before heading out.

8

Stew

After the meal, I made my way to the stable, walking over to where Alex had said to meet. It looked different than it had the night before, with its strong wooden beams highlighted by the sun's rays now. And a few barrels of hay lay outside too, which I hadn't noticed in the dark night. There were at least ten horses in the stable, each its own unique shade of brown, gold, or grey and peacefully standing together. I wished people could get along like that.

I took a deep breath once I saw Alex, determined to find out who these "Watcher people" really were. But, in the back of my mind, I felt a little nervous. After all, my newly mysterious actions were causing August to worry about me, which was the last thing I wanted. But I shrugged this off. Now was my chance to know the truth. As I approached the horses, I realized Alex was hard at work, brushing down one of our horses. "It's a beautiful day for a ride, isn't it," he said contentedly. "Don't you just love Saturdays?"

"Why were you ignoring me at breakfast?" I asked. He looked surprised.

"I wasn't ignoring you. I was just trying to lay low, you know? It's not like anyone can know that we left the Dome after hours," he replied, slyly. Prompty, he swung himself onto his horse.

"I guess that's true," I replied, looking to select a good horse. "So, what's going on with those, um, Watchers?"

"We can't talk about that here," he snapped. "You never know who is part of that!" At that moment, my uncle appeared.

"Princess!" he said, bowing to me.

"Uncle," I replied, curtsying.

"Where are you off to today, Arabella?" I hesitated. "You know I must ask, and be sure you are safe," he added. "I swore to the king himself that I would make sure you are taken care of."

"Just going for a ride with friends, Uncle," I answered. He looked from me to Alex suspiciously. At that moment, Crystal appeared all giddy, with her brown cloak covering her gown and out of breath.

"Hey guys, don't leave without me! I'm here! " she yelled as she ran over, "Ready to see you some more Mel—"

"Meadows! Yes, they will be quite lovely!" Alex said, louder than he was probably hoping to. Crystal looked over, saw her father looking at her, and her eyes grew wide. *Hmph. She can't hide her emotions either.*

"Crystal! I'm glad to see you are here," Uncle continued. "Be sure to keep an eye out for your cousin now," he added, glancing quickly at Alex. I guess he thought he looked suspect or something.

"Yeah Dad!" she agreed quickly, hoping to bring down any suspicion that we were up to something not allowed, namely being involved with leaving Cyrote and heading back to the Melindan island.

He tilted his head down slowly. "Very well." And then to me, "Good day, Princess." He bowed before turning carefully on his cane and trudging back inside. After he entered the Dome, we quickly mounted our horses and were off.

The trees formed something like a natural canopy over our heads, with their branches interlocking above us on either side of the path. Light rays peeked through the little cracks between the leaves, while the gentle breeze floated blossoms all around. It was the perfect day for a ride. When we were almost to the Melindan dock, I figured I could bring up my subject.

"So... are you going to finish your story from last night?" I asked Alex impatiently.

He chuckled. "You always have an agenda, don't you?" I furrowed my eyebrows at him. "Okay, sorry. What I was trying to say before Mr. Green Eyes showed up is that of *course* they were just trying to get to me to get to you."

I let out a deep breath. "Because I'm a Melindan destined for the throne, isn't it?" He nodded his head slowly, looking a bit uncomfortable and guilty for the truth of the matter. Rage quietly began boiling in the pit of my gut. I hated this. *Why can't I ever win?* Without thinking, I sped up ahead of them and crossed the thin dock, before quickly jumping down and running up the hill.

I didn't even know where I was going, but I didn't stop. Ignoring the yelling of my friends after me, I rushed up the hill, leaving my horsy-horse behind. Leaves and palm branches suddenly became another obstacle I pushed away like everything else. I tripped a few times on some uneven rocks and clay in the path but I just kept going. Soon enough, I reached a clearing at the top. It looked out over the entire countryside of my people. Surveying the land, you could see dots of color peeking out between the trees, vibrant protests to the oppression we had placed on them. Equally apparent were the broken down shacks they were living in, poor shadows of the castles we occupied not more than a mile away.

It was all too much for me. I dropped to my hands and knees and just yelled out, letting my voice travel over the edge of the cliff I was at. I wished I could get the frustration of my soul all out at once. Crouched there, looking at all of the injustice my own family had helped to create, it was too much to take in. My fists gathered the clay around me, giving me some grounding. Hot tears stained my cheeks now, running down between my clenched teeth. It felt like even the clay was warming up.

Who was I? My family had ruled this land for hundreds of years and never blinked an eye. Yet I couldn't even stomach what we were doing to stay on top because I am also one of the ones they try to hold down. I don't even think they consider me to be one of them. Half Melindan, all Melindan. Never mind I've barely *met* a Melindan. Forget my father, forget my bloodline going back to the original Bysentor. All they saw was my skin. A threat to their power, to their world where *they* are on top. They couldn't bear to see even a half-Melindan occupy the throne.

Opening my eyes and looking out over the cliff's edge, my breaths became more and more shallow. Someone was coming to get me, no dragging me to the edge. I felt his grip beckoning me closer, forcing me to look out off of its heights to face my watery death. He prepared to throw me off and then, nothing. I crouched there, head wrapped in my arms, shaking violently, not knowing what was happening to my body or where these visions were coming from. I wept softly. Suddenly, I heard the crunching of feet near me. I looked up abruptly to see an old woman in the distance, soft wrinkle lines just beginning to outline her face. She had long, grey hair, elegantly braided into three strong ropes. When she saw me, she began approaching slowly.

"*Mana?*" she called out to me gingerly. "*Mana?*" She came closer now. I stayed very still, just watching her approach me. I really couldn't move. "*Mana, ye le?*" she asked again.

"I'm sorry," I stammered, sitting up a little, sniffling as a few more tears began to form. "I'm not... I don't speak..."

She scrunched her eyebrows and tried again in English. "Dear?" she asked, kneeling next to me and placing a gentle hand on my shoulder. I didn't resist. "Dear, are you alright?"

I looked into her kind face, her warm brown eyes staring into my own. I smiled weakly. "I'm okay," I replied finally. She began to look in wonder at my intricate gown, starting now to get soiled in the mud. We hadn't made time to change before coming today.

At that moment, Alex and Crystal came through the

clearing, both as regally dressed as I. "Arabella!" Alex called out, running over to me.

"Stay back!" the elderly woman shouted. "Get away from us. Your kind is not welcome here!" I turned to her quickly. He stopped abruptly.

"No, it's okay! They are my friends!"

But she didn't listen. Instead, taking a small knife from her pocket, she pointed it at him. "Leave us! The poor girl is in need of help, can you not see? She has caused no trouble." That's when Alex raised his hands in the air and spread his palms apart widely. Then he slowly lowered himself down on one knee.

"*Ye ley!*" he called to her. "We are peaceful!" Crystal, all the while, was frozen in fear at the beginning of the forest's clearing.

The woman paused, squinting at him, and then she dropped her pocket knife. "Mana?" she whispered. "Is that you?" After pausing to look him over, she ran over to Alex and embraced him.

"*Ye ley*, Mana!" she cried out, choking on a few tears. She kissed his forehead and cheeks now and helped him to stand.

"*Ye ley*, Godmother," he said, beaming. She took his hands now and looked up into his face.

"What are you doing here in the forest, Mana, dressed like this?" she shook her head and clicked her tongue. "And with a Melindan in your company?" she asked, confused yet beaming.

"I am here with my friends, Godmother. Come, meet them!" He held out an arm, motioning for us to join him. Slowly, we approached her. To us, he said, "This is my godmother, Peila. I spent a lot of time with them until we moved to another province when I turned fifteen," he recalled somewhat painfully.

"It has really been too long!" she exclaimed to him. "And what are your names?" she asked, looking at me and Crystal now. First, she placed her hands on Crystal's shoulders.

"I'm Crystal, Miss!" she piped sweetly.

"Crystal," she replied. "You are so precious!" Now, she cupped her hands around my cheeks. "And who are *you*?"

I blushed. "I'm Arabella. Arabella Bysentor."

"The Princess? Here among us? *Oye nani!*" she exclaimed.

"Yes, and this is Crystal Bysentor," I added, smiling a little more now and wiping away my tears.

"Wha—why are we all out here?" she stammered. "You royals and me? *Oye nani!* Inside we go!" And with that, she spun around back in the direction she had appeared from. Shrugging his shoulders, Alex followed.

"Come on guys. Don't make her repeat herself," he chuckled. Quickly, we followed him down the stony path through another part of the island. Soon enough, we were in her neighborhood, a modest collection of shacks, each made of the same sturdy wood of which the tavern was constructed. Even so, they were greatly worn, with holes and cracks betraying their age. She beckoned us inside her home, and somehow, it looked much bigger and much homier. A large table and chairs were placed in the center, with a stove and wash bin on the left and a cot on the dirt floor on the right. A beautiful cloth hung across the back wall.

"Did you make that?" I asked her, blinking profusely. "It's

absolutely beautiful," I continued in wonder, my jaw dropping.

"I like her," she said, poking my arm, and winking at Alex. His eyes widened and his cheeks flushed.

"*Mana!*"

She shook her head, chuckling. "It was my mother's," she explained to me. "She was an incredible weaver and..." She paused, looking at me fondly. "Are you sure you haven't been here before?"

I felt a little panicked, thinking about our adventure the previous night. "Why do you ask?"

"You just... perhaps you remind me of someone." she said, shrugging it off. At least I hadn't been recognized from last night. She continued, "Now, are you all hungry?" All of our faces lit up. My stomach called out to me loudly. But Crystal ruined the moment.

"I'm sure we should be getting back now," she said. "Perhaps it's late." I could tell she just felt bad about taking this woman's food.

"Nonsense!" she replied. "I could never let my guests leave hungry!" She clicked her tongue in disapproval. "Hmph! You all are in luck. I made extra today!"

With that, Alex shrugged his shoulders and sat down. I guess he wasn't really one to refuse food. Crystal and I followed suit. A moment later, we each had fat bowls of some kind of stew— a thick, well-seasoned something in front of us. It smelled amazing. She even served us tea, explaining to us how she made it with herbs from her garden.

"This smells incredible," I said, looking at the bowl astonished.

"Oh, it's just something my mother showed me," she said, flipping her hand down. "It's a Melindan dish made with lamb, curry spices, and rice. A staple really."

Alex was already digging in. "Ah— lave— this— shtuff," he managed to get out between mouthfuls.

"It's so delicious," Crystal added, practically swooning over her meal.

"Crowd favorite," Godmother giggled. "Always knocks 'em dead." Then she turned to me confused. "Are you sure you don't know this?" I froze. I knew nothing of these people, except that I was supposedly one of them. In that moment, shame washed over me. Even Alex knew of my food and culture and I didn't even know what 'spice' was.

"Oh," she said, looking at me again. "It's okay if you haven't been taught our way. Everyone starts somewhere." She touched my hand. "You don't have to be afraid, you know? No one is going to laugh at you."

"Thank you," I said, smiling softly.

"Now," she added, "How long have you and Alex been together?" We looked at each other.

"No!" "—It's not like that!" "We just—" The two of us shouting over each other, unable to get the words out fast enough.

"I see," she replied, nodding slowly. "Yes, it's much more serious than that. So, when is the wedding? *Mana*, why haven't you invited me?!" she protested.

"No, Godmother!" he exclaimed, holding her hands. "We aren't together. We are just friends."

She nodded again, clicking her tongue. "Too bad," she said.

"You two have something special, I can *see* it in the way you look into each other's—"

"Godmother!" Alex cut her off frantically. "Thank you but no! She has a suitor already." He was really blushing now. I just held my breath, took a sip of the tea, trying really hard not to feel offended by his clear aversion to me and also trying not to break out laughing. *Also, how did he even know I had a thing for August? Was it really that obvious?* Crystal wasn't as successful as me at masking her feelings, and became something of a sputtering, giggling mess. Ignoring her, I looked down surprised to realize the tea was cinnamon flavored, my favorite! At that moment, an older gentleman walked into the room.

"Peila! Is lunch ready yet?" the man asked. Startled at his appearance, Crystal yelped out. My eyes just widened. But Alex did no such thing. Instead, he stood up and whirled around to embrace him.

"Godfather!" he exclaimed. The man was slightly taken aback for a moment, but then burst into a grin amidst his scruffy white beard, his brown skin crinkling forming the only wrinkles he had, around the corners of his eyes.

"Alex, my son!" They enjoyed a hearty embrace before the godfather joined us to eat. Peila came around swiftly, bringing her husband some of the stew. He looked up at her tenderly. "*Mana*, this looks delicious, I don't know how you do it."

"*Oye nani!*" she said in response, flouncing away from him in lover's gest. He shook his head, still smiling. "My Peila is a true gem. Oh! But I've forgotten to introduce myself!" He let out a strong laugh, and then eyed me and Crystal. "My name is Rupert, and I am the humble man of this house!"

I smiled brightly. He seemed so warm and fun-loving, much like Peila, which I guess is why they were a great match for one another. "And who are these lovely ladies?" he asked.

Alex saved us the trouble this time. "These are Crystal and Arabella... Bysentor." He bit his lip.

"And how have we come to entertain the highest youths in our land? This is a great treat for your old Rupert, Alexander! To see a day like this, my table filled with nobility." He shook his head, contented with the thought. Finally, Peila came bringing her own stew bowl. "*Mana*," he said tenderly, turning to her, "You've been serving us so much. I'll do the dishes!" Playfully, he winked at her before rising up to collect our dishes. She smirked at him.

"Thank you," she replied. Turning back to us she asked us what our program was about. The three of us began explaining what we knew so far off our duties and tasks to manage the kingdom's provinces as best as we could before receiving our respective titles to be able to rule.

Rupert let out a chortle from the sink. "You mean they get you all to do their work for free? And this apprenticeship is for *how* long?"

"Basically, yes," Alex replied, with a hint of disdain coloring his voice.

"The whole summer," Crystal added, similar annoyance in her voice.

"Hmph, I'm amazed that they do it," he replied, shaking his head. Suddenly, I felt indignant. How could they talk about our country like that?

"Mr. Rupert Godfather Sir, if I may—"

"Call me Godfather, *Mana*, the boy already does."

"Oh, well, Mr.— or rather, Godfather, I don't approve of the way you're disrespecting our great Promynthia, your own land and people," I replied, lifting my chin now.

"My own land?" Godfather started, with a start. "Alex! What are you teachin' this young woman?"

Alex shook his head furiously.

"I'm not teaching her anything, sir!"

Godfather's eyes widened. "Well that's the problem!" Then he turned to Crystal. "Missy, you know about the real things going on right? I know you're royalty and all but you must know."

She nodded calmly. "Yes, I know, Godfather. The injustice isn't hard to see, and our rulers are the most corrupt—" I turned to her in shock. I couldn't believe what I was hearing.

"Crystal! How could you talk this way about your own father?" I exclaimed.

"Bella, it's just politics! Don't tell me your parents never told you the truth of what they have to do?"

"Told me what, Crystal? My parents are doing everything they can to make life better for us. And you Melindans should be grateful for all we're doing for you!" With that, I slammed my hands on the table angrily and stood up. I must have slapped them too hard because they felt like they were on fire. I looked down to see the damage, but that's when I saw that the table we were sitting at had split in half.

Bending down with horror, I peered at the severed table, two gashes burned straight down the middle, and burn marks in the shape of... my own hands on either side of the cracked wood. "What... is... HAPPENING!" I screamed, looking to my own hands in horror. They were glowing with yellow, sparkling light, and then slowly began fading to my normal palm color. Everyone else looked up in shock.

Looking from the table to me, Crystal whispered, "So it is true!"

"WHAT'S TRUE?!" I shouted, looking frantically from her to Alex to my new godparents to my sparking hands for answers. I crouched on the ground shaking. What was happening to me? Godmother quickly rushed over to me and held me close in her arms.

"*Mana*, it's quite alright!" she cooed. "It's just your gift, Dear!"

"*Gift*?" I whispered back, wonderingly.

"All Melindans have a gift, Arabella! I mean, how do you think we got such a lovely home?" she asked, pointing her head towards the masterfully made cabin. "Rupert's gift is wood manipulation!" My breaths grew shorter and shorter. "But we aren't allowed to wield anymore, since the government believes our power is a threat. We just do it in secret."

"Oh no!" I said weakly. "I must not have been taking my medicines! My dreams— they're not real— they..."

"Shh, shhhh, *Mana*," Godmother said gently. "It's alright, Arabella, you're just experiencing your gift!" But I refused to listen to her. Still shaking, I quickly stood up and freed myself from her grasp.

"I'm sorry, but this isn't— can't be real." Desperately, I ran outside, feeling very frightened by whatever had just happened. Without looking back, I started racing back down the mountain, back down to normalcy, back down to where everything was right and I was boring.

"Arabella!" Alex shouted after me, running out after me.

"I'm going back to the Dome!" I shouted firmly. Pushing back some branches in my way, I grappled the straps of my my trusty horse, and struggled to mount, but got on and held tight. By this point, he and Crys had of course caught up with me.

"But wait!" he said, holding onto my horse's bridle.

"Let go of my horse, Alex!"

"But Arabella! Haven't you heard of the Melindans' powers?"

"No! It's not real, Alex! This isn't real!" And with that, I tried to get my horse to run, but he was still holding on. Losing my balance, I screamed, realizing I was falling into the water! My brain was on fire as much as my limbs, as I struggled to thrash around and grasp for air. I had never been allowed to learn to swim. *Is this how I die?*

A loud splash to my left was soon to answer that question. Alex had jumped in to save me. I felt his sturdy arm under my armpit as he pulled me back towards the dock and hoisted us both up. By this point, Crystal had caught up with us and was now panicking. "Arabella, are you alright?"

Breathing hard, I stood up and began wringing out my dress. This was just too much. I needed those oils. Without hesitating or looking back, I threw myself onto my horse and bade him to go. I ignored Alex and Crystal yelling behind me desperately to wait, to stop. I squeezed my eyes shut, and focused on getting back home. *Nothing can stop me from getting this crown.* Uncle was right. Even though Melinda was beautiful, I couldn't go back. Wielding, even if it was real, was against the law. In thirty minutes time, I was back at the Dome where I belonged.

That night wasn't much better than earlier. I couldn't even bring myself to eat dinner. Of course, Crystal tried to come and talk to me before bed, but I refused. "I think you should just go to sleep." I suggested, arms crossed in defense across my nightgowned body. Seeing my determination, she turned away glumly to head back to her own chamber. Before completely leaving she replied gently with a shrug, "Well, I hope you're feeling better soon."

I surely hope you do too, I thought. *How could she possibly be going along with the delusion that I could shoot fire out of my hands? That's not natural, and literally makes no sense.* I shuddered, thinking of the possibility that even Crystal and Alex themselves were a figment of my imagination. Feverishly, I rummaged around my drawer to see how much medicine I had left. Of course the vial was almost empty, but luckily there would be more coming for me in a few days. Taking the last dosage I had, I turning over roughly in my covers, settling for a less than restful night sleep.

9

Sunday

The next morning, I hurried to breakfast. I felt optimistic about this day. No magic. No godparents. No trouble. This day was all about fun. And I looked forward to hopefully spending it with the ever intriguing August.

"I trust you had a great night sleep?" he asked me at breakfast. Crystal and Alex were sitting all the way at the other end of the chamber, sort of sullenly looking over to me every now and then. "Arabella?" August asked.

"Oh!" I started. I guess I had been looking at them too long. "Yeah, it was fine. How about yourself?"

"Always good. Um, want me to pass you some tea?" I nodded enthusiastically.

"So, where is my uncle taking us all again?" I asked, trying to ignore my ever louder nagging thoughts.

"My father's palace actually." he replied, shrugging sheepishly. My eyes widened.

"Palace?" I asked.

"Yeah. Since he governs Melinda, his Dome is there. It's not far from here really, about a thirty minute ride or so."

"You don't say?" I replied, pretending not to know how far it was, instead taking a large sip of tea. *So that's how he knows my Uncle.*

"Yup! It's beautiful really, and it contains a lot of history about the place." I smiled, letting him explain. "It's a stunning place and there's so much to see about the Melindans too. I guess... do you know much about them?"

"No, not particularly," I said. "I mean, I am only half."

"Oh, okay. Yeah, I suppose not." he said with a wave of his hands, popping another spoonful of eggs into his mouth. I scrunched my eyebrows taking in those words. *What did he mean by that? I mean, of course I'm one of them, right? I mean... at least half of one? Sometimes one half too much.* I sighed.

Seeing my discomfort he added, "But don't worry! It's not like I see you as being *like* them. I know you're different," he said with a smile. That didn't really make me feel much better. I thought of the sweetness of Peila and Rupert. *Would I really want to be so different than them?* Confused, I brushed it aside.

Within a short time, the servants had us all hitched on a long, wide coach, with multiple horses at the front of our coach. "Let's get on with it, noblefolk!" Uncle shouted. "The Dome doesn't have all day to wait for us!" Quickly, we shuffled on and were on our way. August and I spoke of war theories and historical trends we found interesting in recent times. The time seemed to fly by to me, and I could tell he was having a good time as well. Once we had all dismounted, it was time for us to explore his father's home. It truly looked grandiose to me. Somehow, it was more breathtaking than I had imagined- honestly, it was more breathtaking than even the Dome of Cyrote.

First of all, it was at least twice the height. And secondly, its placement made it look even more impressive. The Dome sat atop a tall cliff that hovered over the Melindan peninsula. In fact, it was basically sitting on a giant precipice looming over it like some sort of ever watching guard. This was especially easy to note given the multiple guards dressed completely in an elegant white, who marched around the Dome's precarious edge facing the peninsula. Some came out of the Dome to relieve the current ones from their post, and those guards gratefully let them, clearly exhausted from their long night shifts. I scrunched my eyebrows thinking about it. *Why would people as poor as the Melindans need constant watching like that? I mean, it's not like they were causing trouble or shooting fire out of their hands... right?* Before we were able to leave and before I could assure myself that I was just being silly, Uncle Jacob had stood up in front of the coach in order to give us his 'please be safe' speech.

"Please be safe, everyone." (Told you.) "This is a good opportunity for you all to explore the grounds here as well as speak with the assistants and nobility about this Dome. Do not do anything you will regret." He cleared his throat, muttering under his breath, "Or anything I would regret."

Continuing on, he added, "And, as some of you may know, this province oversees the affairs of the Melindans, so make sure to see how it is governed. Looking down at the poorest and weakest of our peoples should give you all ideas on how to help your own provinces. Learn from the worst and help the best!" At this point, everyone on the coach glared back at me. I smiled weakly. *Well, we can't all be winners, can we?* I thought in response, perturbed by the extra attention. "Likewise, remember that it is August Frederick's own father that is in charge of this grand estate, so perhaps August can assist you with some of your questions as well." At this point, they all shifted their grimaces from me to August and nodded at him. Some of the girls even winked! I rolled my eyes. "Be back at the coach at 5 pm!" Scarcely had he finished when the entire lot of us began chatting and heading out excitedly.

"Come on!" August said, grabbing my wrist and hurrying off the coach. It was all I could do to keep up and ignore the angry faces of the other girls offended by his lack of attention to them.

"Where are we going?" I asked, giggling and struggling to run alongside due to my dang skirt. He looked back at me, excitement in his eyes.

"We're at my home today. Where *aren't* we going today?" he asked, shrugging his shoulders.

I let out a laugh, throwing my head back. "Okay, you lead the way!" In a matter of minutes, we found ourselves wandering around inside. The Dome of Walabe was much bigger than the Dome of Cyrote. August showed me the multiple bedrooms, servant quarters, the huge kitchen, the prison chambers (which were filled with a lot of people who looked a lot like me...), the upper rooms, the lower rooms, and even intricately built areas for storing food in the cellar. The Fredericks seemed to have had multiple extensions made to the base circular building structure. In fact, the two rectangular flanks installed on each side of the Dome in an L shape basically tripled the amount of space in there.

"Well, what do you think of it?" he asked me, when we neared the end of the tour.

"I don't know what to say— it's actually getting close to the size of my castle!"

"What? We're giving you all competition?" he said incredulously and then, shaking his head, added, "Let's just say my father has big taste." I smiled at him. His father seemed almost as extra as he was.

After that we headed to the top of the Dome for lunch with the rest of the nobles. Of *course*, there was an extra dining chamber installed up there. And lucky for me, there were multiple umbrellas at the tables, because... well, of course I forgot mine again.

Lunch was pretty delicious. It featured little sandwiches rolled up into bite-sized pieces, a delicious lemon and sugar water drink and small cakes of pumpernickel muffins for dessert. What was most interesting to me, though, was a special "local" food they had featured for anyone to try. It was called "Melindan Stew" and was in a self-serve station to the side of the chamber along with extra lemon water juice. It was even completed with little palm tree cutouts and pineapples, which I guess were supposed to mimic the island's vibes. This honestly surprised me. *Why would anyone want to eat anything labeled Melindan?* Yet everyone had some. In fact, they had to bring out a second bowl of it just to accommodate the demand! Curious, I decided to try it and see what all of the hubbub was about.

Walking over to the station, I peered into the bowl to find a delicious smelling soup. It looked a whole lot like the one Peila had made for us. For a moment, I felt a pang of sadness come over me. *Why did I miss them? I really just met them!* A tap on my shoulder interrupted my thoughts. "Couldn't stay away from the stew, huh?" Alex said, grinning at me. I shook my head, disappointed at myself.

"I guess not," I replied, shrugging my shoulders. As if on cue, Crystal came skipping over at this point. "Hey guys!" she squealed. "I wonder how bad this one will be?" I looked back at her.

"Bad?"

"You don't *really* expect them to make the soup right, do you?" she asked. I stared at her blankly. I don't know, I guess I never really encountered this sort of thing before.

"She means that this is clearly not authentic Melindan food," Alex chimed in. "They can't make it too much like the real thing." Looking over his shoulder, he then cupped his hand to his mouth and whispered, "I don't think they can handle that much flavor!" The three of us burst out laughing. I was intrigued now, and greedily got myself a generous helping.

"Well, here I go!" I exclaimed, scooping a big, heaping spoonful into my face. That's when I burst out laughing and may or may not have accidentally lost some of my food on the stone ground...

"Arabella! What is wrong with you?" Alex managed between choking laughs.

Catching my breath and swallowing, I defended myself. "I'm sorry! I just really thought that it would be sort of good." Crystal shook her head, still giggling. I kept going. "It was literally just like a brown sauce over dried chicken with no flavor other than salt!"

Nodding her head, Crystal added, "Yep, that's about right!"

"How could they serve this? How is this even *legal?*"

"I don't know, ask your dad!" Alex retorted. At that, I looked up from my laughter in amazement. There everyone was, eating this terrible fraud they called "Melindan Stew" and just really enjoying it. It was like they wanted a taste of something different without having to commit. Like they wanted an experience without any of the history or people attached. I mean, we were literally eating right on top of the island with a zillion guards keeping them from ever crossing their island border, lest their evil dark spices taint our driest of chicken.

Our laughter dying down, the three of us were left staring at each other in silence. Crystal broke it. "So, how have you been?" This was so annoying, I had only been avoiding them for maybe 24 hours and they were already acting so weird.

"Guys, I'm fine," I replied. She and Alex exchanged nervous looks.

"Well, Bella, it's just that—"

"Just that what, *Crys*? You're worried I'm still wet from the sea or something?"

"Well..." she paused and took a deep breath. "We think that your powers are real." My eyes dimmed, and I felt anger beginning to pit in my stomach. I balled my fists.

"Listen!" I said, a little more forcefully than I meant to. "For once in my life, I'm starting to seem semi-normal and you two seem to want to take that away from me!"

"But Bella—"

"No!" And then I added, "Come with me." It was time for

me to explain something to these two Melindan sympathizers. At that moment August looked up at me, waving frantically from his seat. His face looked happy but concerned. I gave him a cheery grin so he would know everything was okay. Then, Crys and Alex followed me into the long stone corridor where no one else could hear. I took a long deep breath before beginning to speak.

"I can see I'm going to have to explain something to you about my life, about being a Melindan." I looked up at them, looking for them to leave, but they just stared at me, beckoning me to continue on. So I did. "When I was eight, I had my Incident. I'll never forget it," I added, shaking my head. "I was playing around the castle all morning in the sun, in the large front yard. I wanted to make a pretend fire like I was camping or surviving or something, so I gathered a bunch of sticks together and pretended to warm them and make a fire.

"Except, I actually made a fire. Like, my hands warmed up and a tiny flame was in the middle of the sticks and brush I had gathered." I swallowed hard. "I didn't know how to stop it," I recalled, my hands beginning to shake. "And so it just grew and *grew*, and started consuming the grass all around me.

"One of the servants saw me out there and called the guards instead of my parents, assuming I was some Melindancausing trouble. And that's when they tied my hands and threw me in our prison. No questions were asked." Tears were starting to run down my face now. Crystal wrapped me in her arms then, trying to comfort me. I recalled myself desperately crying out to the guards dragging me to the cell that I was the king's daughter, Arabella Bysentor. They ignored my frantic screams.

"No one even noticed that I was gone. Later that night, a strange guard I'd never seen before, who was dressed in all white robes, dragged me out from the cell to the top of the castle. He threatened to push me off of the roof when... that power kicked in again and saved me. Somehow, I burned him and he went tumbling off the roof! At that moment, more guards and my parents came running up to the roof, realizing that there had been a mistake and that the white-robed guard was not one of us. They found me there crying and shaking, and picked me back up." I looked over at Alex and Crystal now, who were both somberly listening to my story and nodding their heads.

I took a deep breath again, shaking my head. "After that, my mother forbid me from ever leaving the castle without permission. She shielded me so much she didn't even want my *skin* touching the sun, which is why I'm always supposed to use umbrellas. My parents never wanted anything bad happening to me again. Even my Uncle Jacob who was living with us at the time moved to his own dome, Cyrote. He hoped giving me more space would help me forget it all." I shrugged. "I guess since I kept having nightmares about the Incident, they told me none of it was real and gave me weird oils and stuff to make me forget." I shook my head. "The worst part of it all," I finally admitted at a whisper, "is that I'm afraid that if others find out, they'll see me... as a monster." I couldn't believe I actually said that out loud.

Alex put a firm hand on my shoulder. "I'm sorry that happened to you, Bella," he said softly.

"Yeah" I replied, barely above a whisper.

"And, we don't see you or any Melindan that way at all, Bella!" Crys added emphatically pulling me in for a quick hug.

"But Arabella, do you want to know how to use that power though?" Alex asked me gently, adding a hand to my shoulder. I blinked back tears to look up at him. "I completely understand if you don't, but, I feel like now would be your opportunity more than ever." I took a moment to think about it, and looked fondly at these two wild people I called friends. Probably the first I'd ever had.

"Bella?" August called out, coming from behind a pillar or something.

"August!" I exclaimed, hands feeling sweaty. "Were you here the whole time?"

"What? No, Bella, I just saw you walking over here and wanted to make sure you were okay," he replied, now looking a little suspiciously at me, Crys and Alex awkwardly huddled in this back corner of his home.

"Oh!" I replied, grabbing his arm and wiping away my remaining tears on my sleeve. "Everything's perfectly fine!"

"Okay," he said, smiling at me, but looking with disdain on my other friends. I hoped he didn't hear the monster part. One more time, I turned back to Crystal and Alex, who were both earnestly looking at me, almost with a worried look in their eyes. I tried to dissuade them without making August seem any more suspicious. "Sorry, guys," I said casually and shrugging, "now's just not the right time."

10

Dome

After that trip to Walabe, August and I found ourselves going there more often. I think this was the perfect thing to do. This was the best way for me to really start avoiding Crys and Alex without me feeling as awkward. I don't know if I wanted to spend too much time in Cyrote anymore anyway. Even just seeing those two reminded me of the powers I was trying to forget. But for some reason, I couldn't bring myself to take those oils anymore, even if they were helpful with me forgetting and suppressing the powers. I guess I just couldn't fully deny it anymore, now that I knew the real truth. I settled for using willpower to keep them down.

The Dome turned out to be a great place to get work done— well, that is, when others weren't frequenting the premises. We appreciated the chance to get out of Cyrote and able to really work on our project in the place that overlooked the very city we were impacting, Melinda. Plus, I didn't mind the extra time I got to spend with August.

Per his suggestion, we found ourselves often on the roof

of one of the Dome's extensions. It was often so sunny and bright there, and I appreciated its overlook of the entire city. On the horizon were long stretches of dark green mountaintops overlapping one another and only bested by an ever increasing light blue sky. Often there were wisps of white that helped to break up the expanse a little. And in the foreground was the mount where the Melindans lived. From this height, I could see the island perfectly. It was such a good groove, it was hard to believe that we'd been in the apprenticeship for a whole month.

I appreciated the fresh air, as it really helped me with thinking about suggestions for this people. I always felt tickled by seeing all of the colors that dotted the otherwise bushy green peninsula- they were tapestries from the Melindan homes. Smiling to myself, I wondered if Peila and Rupert could see me from here. But then a sick feeling replaced that. Did Melindans ever even look at the Dome or come here, or did they feel isolated and trapped on their little makeshift island?

"August?" I asked as we were sitting there, just getting out our things for the day. "Have you ever seen Melindans in your home before?"

He wrinkled his nose. "Melindans? Um," he paused. "Well, yes. You!"

I rolled my eyes. "No, *besides* me. I don't think I've ever seen them come here."

He nodded slowly, furrowing his brows. "You're definitely right. I don't know how I've never noticed that before."

I shrugged. "Maybe because it doesn't affect you." An awkward pause followed, so I just filled in the space. "Um, but are they welcome here? As in, are they allowed at the Dome?"

His eyes widened. "Of course they are! Every Promynthian is welcome at the Domes. They are the symbol of our communities! You know each province has a dome like a communal home for everyone to visit, meet their nobles, and have fun."

Now it was my turn to furrow my brows. "Well then, if it's open to everyone, then why don't Melindans ever come? Gosh, I didn't even know they were *allowed*!"

"Why not?"

"August, everybody follows context clues," I said, rolling my eyes again. "I mean, seriously, if you're a hated people and no one who looks like you or dresses like you ever comes to anything officially 'Promynthian' and nothing that represents you is in that place, why would you come?"

"Who said Melindans are hated?"

"You don't have to *say* it— it's written all over these white-washed stones!"

"I can't believe this!"

"Seriously?"

"Yes, Bella, I'm serious! No wonder your father married your mother. He was trying to help Promynthia know your people are accepted."

I nodded my head, adding under my breath as he became lost in thought... "It's about time, no one who looked like us was ever in the palace before..."

"Bella! We have to *do* something about this!"

I squinted my eyes at him. "Isn't that what this whole apprenticeship is about?"

He shook his head vehemently. "Not at first. I thought that these people just needed some programs to maybe feed them or give them some proper clothing or something—"

Proper what now? Wait, he's still going, listen up!

"But now I realize that the truth is that they need to realize their real place in our Promynthian society. They need to know that they are one of us!"

I smiled at him. At least he tried. Reaching out for his hand, I ventured to ask, "And... how do you want to try to do that?"

He held onto mine too, eyeing me excitedly. "By inviting them to the Dome of course!"

I nodded slowly. "Wow."

"What?"

"I mean, I guess that's just really bold! Great idea, it's just so different than how things usually are."

"Well, that's the point isn't it?"

"Yeah!" I agreed, nodding quickly. But then I stopped. "Wait, what about how they will feel?"

"What do you mean?"

"As in, won't they feel out of place or something?"

"Oh," he replied, sighing now. "I guess I forgot about that part. Maybe... hmm, maybe we can just decorate the Dome to be a little more Melindan!"

"Wow! Well, that would be really something and probably work," I guessed, shrugging my shoulders.

"Yes, it will!" He agreed raising his hand to my shoulder. "And you'll be just the one to teach us."

I shifted my eyes from side to side, confused. "Um, August, I haven't really, you know, hung out with Melindans before." *At least not really. Can you hardly count the tavern or the flame throwing and table destroying?* "Are you sure you don't want to consult, I don't know, a *real* Melindan or something?"

"No, no, it'll be fine," he replied. "It'll be easier to just talk to you anyway. Besides, I'm sure it just flows through your veins. You'll know what to do!"

I smiled nervously. Well, I did have a few ideas. Hopefully they would work out.

II

Tuesday

Luckily we still had a few days left before the actual event, so naturally, I used my time to bury my nerves and try distracting myself from every feeling possible. And since I was still determining to avoid Crys and Alex, I had to try my hand at making other... friends. As in, people who didn't already seem to outright accept me on Day 1 of this whole apprenticeship thingy. I would have to be smooth, cool, coy, and fresh. All of which I was perfectly terrible at doing, so I knew this would be a complete success.

"Darling!" I called out to Tiffany at lunch, sauntering coolly over to her as I held my bowl of tomato soup. Just then, I saw August in my line of sight. He shrugged his shoulders and gave a soft wave. A feeling in the pit of my stomach reminded me how guilty I felt for avoiding them.

"Dear!" Tiffany called out then, waving a dark silky gloved hand in my direction frantically and interrupting my guilty thoughts. *Why is she wearing gloves to lunch?* "Come, come," she ordered, motioning me to sit by her. Taking a deep breath, I turned away from August's gaze to smile brightly at Tiffany, quickly sitting down beside her. "Now," she began, once she saw I was settled with my plate, "you *must* tell me how your project is going."

"Oh, right," I said, beginning to stall by sipping some tomato soup with my spoon.

"Yes, tell me, how can you manage with your... um, *clientele*?" she added, a concerned, plastic look in her cheeks.

"Well, um," I tried, but got sort of choked on the amount of fakeness that was in her words, and I started coughing on my bit of soup. Panicked, I reached for a cloth napkin to cover my mouth and my now blushing cheeks! *Get it together, Arabella! Be smooth.* "Mm hmm!" I said forcefully, clearing my throat. "Yes, it's been quite the adventure for me."

"And?"

"And what?"

"Well, what *kind* of adventure is it? I mean, luckily for me, I get to work with the Epitomans, who are poised, quiet, dignified. I mean with their good salaries and high culture, I barely even have anything to do. But for you, dealing with those backward dark creatures— I mean, how are you even able to deal with them?"

That was the wrong thing to say. My face dropped. "What do you mean, *Tiffany*? They're just people, right? Which means it's just like ruling over anyone else."

Now her face dropped and stared straight into my soul. Act dropped. "Maybe it's because you're just like them," she hissed. But before she could spew out any more poison, Mr. Green Eyes interrupted and sat right next to me.

"Afternoon, ladies," he cooed, grinning a little too much in my direction for subtlety. Tiffany, clearly perturbed, squinted at me quickly before plastering on that too-wide smile again.

"August, how are you?" she asked slyly, placing a hand on his arm softly.

He looked down slightly surprised, but didn't move from her touch. Instead, he looked over at me and replied, "Just having the best day possible with my partner." I could have fallen over from the butterflies collecting in my stomach. I smiled at him weakly, before realizing I was still sitting in front of this ticking time bomb of a girl. So, I tried brushing it off, pretending his words were casual.

"Yeah, August and I just like to hang out at his Dome to get good work done."

"Oh really?" she squeaked in an eerily cheerful voice. "And what do you do when you aren't working?" My eyes widened in shock. Luckily, August came to the rescue.

"It's not like that, Tiff," he said calmly, shaking his head. "We really just enjoy the atmosphere of being close to the people we're serving," he added with a shrug. I nodded slowly, trying to look sincere. I couldn't believe what I was doing. This was just so tiring— all of the small talk and the fake smiles and me trying so hard not to just tell this girl off completely. I thought about Crystal, and how much more fun I would be having if I was sitting with her right now instead of Tiffany. Audibly, I sighed.

"What's that, Bell?" Tiff asked forebodingly.

"Oh, nothing!" I said quickly. *Internal sigh.*

12

Show

Before we knew it, the day of our Dome Event had come. It didn't take much to convince the higher-ups in Walabe that this was a good idea in the first place. August ended up doing most of the talking and persuading, since he had the connections, looked the part, yada yada yada. Once we finally got their approval to move forward with our project, the real work of getting the Dome ready for Melindan visitors began.

Surprisingly, the easiest part turned out to be disseminating the information about our event to the Melindans. Since the guards were regularly patrolling the island, August got the clear to have them post scrolls around with the information of our event. I felt proud thinking about all of our little flyers being there to make people feel welcomed to their Dome. *They'll feel as Promynthian as ever*, I thought to myself, smiling. Although amidst my pride, I also felt a little worried. *What if they didn't come? Would that affect how Uncle Jacob saw our work?* I hoped that he would at least see the effort we put into our event to know that we were making the right connections, spreading out our information, and inviting our assigned city to attend. I hoped that he would give us some extra leniency since we were dealing with Melindans. Contrary to what everyone else assumed, I was no more familiar with these people than they were. I truly had no idea if they would respond to something like this. It didn't take long for me to find out how they would respond, because the fourteenth of July came much earlier than I expected. I guess that's the way things go when you're planning an event. It just sneaks up on you before you're even ready for it!

"Relax, Bella!" August had reassured me earlier that morning, placing his strong hands around my shoulders to stop me from pacing back and forth in the hallway.

"I am relaxed!" I retorted.

"Sure," he replied, chuckling. I simply crossed my arms. (I was fine.) With a half-smile, he dared to focus those grass green eyes into my heart until it started melting. *Don't give in, Arabella.* But I couldn't resist the dreaminess, not even for a moment.

"Fine!" I confessed, thrusting my chin into the air. "You're right. I'm scared!"

"Why? Everything is going to go well. There's nothing to worry about," he said without moving his hands from their comforting position resting on me.

I cocked my head to the side now. "And why not?"

"Because," he replied, shrugging his shoulders, "they've got the smartest, prettiest woman in charge of the whole thing."

My face began to feel warm. "Yeah?" I asked, looking down now, trying to swallow my smile.

Gently he placed my flyaway curl behind my ear. "Really,"

he said earnestly. "And I'll be right there with you the whole time." He reached for my hands now reassuringly. I squeezed them gratefully, hoping to get rid of some nerves as well.

Thirty minutes later, the Dome of Walabe opened for the special appearance of the Melindans. People began pouring in, and honestly, I was surprised at how many of them there were. I guess I just didn't expect that many Melindans to be into history for some reason. But here they were, coming in as families and friends, eager to come to the place where they probably weren't welcome before.

The servants did a great job of creating a logical flow through the museum, and allowed families in a few at a time so that the place wouldn't get overcrowded. In a matter of thirty minutes, the place was completely packed. August and I walked around arm-in-arm to greet people and let them know that we were happy to see them here. I wore a red, velvet dress with puffed sleeves and black mesh layers at the bottom, hoping to look the part of princess so that they would feel more assured of my authority. I even straightened my hair to look more official. As usual, it doubled in length, from my shoulders to well down my back. I always forgot how long it truly was! August didn't have to try very much to look regal. *I guess certain skin always looks right in a suit and tie.*

Nonetheless, people looked happy to see us, and they wanted me to hold their babies and give them blessings and whatnot. I was surprised though. This was my first public event, but it felt nothing like the ones my parents held for Promynthians when I was a child. There was something powerful about seeing so many people who looked like *me* in one place. These people were all shades of tan and brown, happily bouncing around with curls like mine or braided locks like the waitress from my first night in the tavern. Their smiles were bright and kind, and their skin was glowing in the sunlight.

Everything from the exhibits to the ice cream shop was filled with Melindans learning about how the Dome worked and related to their lives. I hoped they appreciated the tapestries I'd placed around. Truthfully, I didn't really know very much about Melindans at all. *What things about our history did I not know? Maybe I could ask Peila... but, I remembered that we wouldn't be talking because I would not discuss those "powers" with her.* Shaking it off, I came back to the present moment, and smiled again at the crowds.

August and I began speaking to an older gentleman with a cane and a lot to say. But all of a sudden, we heard rumblings on the Dome grounds. I looked up, out through the open doors, wondering what in the world I was hearing. August, with wide eyes, gripped my shoulders tightly. I looked at him, "Is everything alright—"

"Get back!" a guard outside shouted. He and several others pointed their semi-automated arrows towards the narrow path leading to the Dome while others began hurrying the people inside and to the back of the building. Just before the doors shut, I caught a glimpse of white robed soldiers marching up like an army before them. They had their own arrows and began shooting then at the Dome! Screams filled the room as people took a mad rush to the back patio for cover. August dragged me away from the crowd and took us to higher ground where we could hide.

"August, what's happening!" I yelled over the confusion, tripping over my dress and trying to keep up with his pull.

"Get to the top! It's an attack!" he yelled back. We ran up the stairs to a secret tunnel opening in the wall on the second floor. Once there, we joined his father. Where we stood, we could actually see down to the first floor through the glass ceiling. The guards had successfully pushed most people out to the gardens and rooftop eating area, but there was a funnel backup, where people were still rushing to get through the narrow door leading outside. And the white-robed soldiers had just penetrated inside. Helplessly, we stood there, watching what was happening. I felt completely powerless to stop it, and blinked back tears of frustration. *What was being done to protect the people down there?*

Now that the coup was inside, there was nothing to shield those who hadn't made it outside yet. They mercilessly pointed their arrows at them. I held my breath, not wanting to accept a slaughter. At that moment, the old man we had spoken to, rushed out from the crowd to distract them.

"Stay back, ya fools!" was all he could muster, as he swung his cane at one of them. Merciless, a soldier shot an arrow right through his chest. I screamed. August held me tightly, trying to muffle my cries. That's when I realized our hiding spot wasn't sound-proof. The same soldier signaled to a few others, who brought a cannon over and pointed it at the sealing. Before August could push me out of the way, a hole was blown through the ceiling, cracking the glass and sending the chandelier directly below it shattering to the ground. I was too close to the edge, stunned from shock and fear. I fell through the ceiling yelping for life and closing my eyes. But when I opened them, I was... floating? I was hovering over the shards of glass, suspended by streams of fire in my hands. Not knowing how, I dropped gracefully to the ground. Without thinking about it, I started fighting back.

"You heard him!" I yelled to the coup. "*Get back!*" I screamed, redirecting my fire streams to them. With their uniforms catching on fire, they fell back immediately and started running back down the hill, dropping their scorched arrows as they went. I guess my forbidden dark magic was too forbidden for them. The guards, the people, and August all stood there staring at me for a moment. I looked down at my now sparking hands and dropped to my knees. *How did I do that?*

People began cheering for me and chanting my name. "Princess Arabella! She is merciful! She is our queen!" They crowded around me slowly, wanting to see who I was. But I heard them as a noisy blur. All I could think about was the old man who had given me courage and had been attacked by the soldiers. Slowly I looked over to him, and saw him breathing heavily. Hoping for the best, I pulled out the arrow quickly. He cried out in pain, but I just shut my eyes and focused on breathing, while cupping my still-glowing hands over his heart. I don't know why— it just felt right somehow. In a few moments, his cries stopped, and his eyes fluttered open. His shirt was soaking with blood, but his heart was beating and his bleeding had stopped. I looked into his jet black eyes and he gratefully grabbed my hands. "You saved me, *Mana*."

That was about all the crowds could take. They looked at me and at the man, and began swarming around us and asking us questions and continuing their chants. Some women began to help him off of the ground. I still stood there kneeling in the glass and just looked up at August, staring at me with wide eyes through the broken ceiling. I had a lot of explaining to do.

13

Found

"So, let me make sure I'm hearing you right— you've had magical 'powers' your whole life, can shoot fire out of your hands, and you've never told anyone?"

I tilted my head from side to side. "More or less."

"And all Melindans have these powers?"

"I'm not really sure," I lied. Just because I wouldn't be getting in trouble for using them didn't mean they wouldn't.

"And you aren't going to use them?"

"Not necessarily!"

August shook his head emphatically. "I can't believe this, Bella! What's stopping you? You could make the whole country obey you."

"I'm afraid, August! The last time I used them I destroyed everything in my path and almost set myself on fire!"

"No. The last time you used them you set a bunch of rebels on fire and saved a man's life." I thought about that. I guess he was right. *Maybe these powers weren't all bad.* I looked down at my hands and rubbed them feverishly.

"So, you really think I should try and learn to use them?"

He threw up his hands. "All I'm saying is you should figure out how to use them so you can use them right, you know?"

I nodded in agreement. "That's a good point."

He nudged me. "Aaand, when you figure it out, let me know. Maybe we can figure out how to empower these people together. Maybe they aren't such a lost cause after all."

I wrinkled my nose at that. But he nudged me back. "I'm kidding, Bella. But really, you should figure out what you can do and if you're the only one."

I agreed. Something like determination began welling inside of me. Maybe I couldn't be normal, but perhaps I could do something good for these people. Even if it meant looking like a freak, I knew how good it felt to be able to pull that man's life back into his body, how to protect all of those people. If there was something I could do to help them, it was my duty to find out.

The following morning, Crystal, Alex and I headed out to the peninsula. They were more than overjoyed that I had finally decided to embrace this stuff. I felt annoyed more than anything, because they were right and I was wrong. But of course a morning with these two jovial souls wouldn't be complete without a good amount of annoying cheer for that hideous time of day.

"Hey Bell?" Crystal had said softly to me, nudging me ever so slightly with her shoulder.

"Noooo," I'd moaned in response, firmly grasping the pillow around my head in protest. But of course, she continued with her sweet sounds.

"Um, Bella, you're the one who wanted this so…" She drew

out her last word, allowing it to trickle off at the end. I peered up at her in disgust, squinting at her awful morning cheeriness.

"Have you no... shame?" I'd croaked out. She blinked twice, confused. I groaned again, and beneath the covers, managed to muffle out, "Just forget it, I'll just be normal." At this, she immediately turned into a fierce fireball.

"ARABELLA BYSENTOR, get out of bed at once!" She'd snapped, sounding alarmingly like my mother. I snapped awake out of my covers to see her standing before me, fully dressed, arms crossed, and face annoyed. Within five minutes I was ready to go and out the Dome doors.

Finally, the three of us made it to the stables and right on the road to the island. I appreciated the quiet of the early dawn, and soon began to hear some cheerful birds join the cacophony of the morning chorus. Pretty soon the sun would be rising. Now, I may not like mornings, but nothing cheers me up like a good sunrise. Those skies can be just breathtaking, all streaked orange and majestic. I hoped for a good one.

For this trip, Alex broke the silence. "Hey, Arabella," he started. "How... how are you feeling this morning?" I appreciated how much he tried to be casual with his question. Yet, underneath his hesitation I knew he was still worried we weren't on good terms since he was taking me *way* out of my comfort zone. I figured I'd wait a bit before reassuring him.

"Tired," I replied, sighing. "You?" He glared at me. Satisfied with his clearly annoyed response, I grinned back before conceding. "Okay, okay, you win!" I chuckled, shaking my head. "I'm nervous, okay!" I looked down at my horse, beginning to stroke his beautiful golden mane, and let the insecurity well up inside of me. "I'm terrified." I closed my eyes, not wanting to believe myself. But it was true. *Who was I trying to fool? Obviously I wasn't anyone worth training or anything.* The biggest hope I'd had for myself was to disappear and just blend into the background. Yet here I was, about to stick out more than I ever had before. How was I supposed to feel?

Alex maneuvered his horse so he could ride right next to me. Then he reached over and touched my hand softly. "You're going to do amazing," he said with so much belief that it startled me. Grateful, I gave a half smile back.

Within the hour, we were back at the mountain clearing where I had first broken down and tied our horses to the trees. At least I had that time as well as the ten minute walk up the dirt road to think before I had to face Peila and Rupert again. I was going to need all the help I could get. But, stalling doesn't stop things from eventually happening, so there we were about to knock on the door to their home when Peila opened it up grinning at us.

She beamed at me and flashed a big smile, as if she already knew I would return all along. "Ready?"

Before I knew what was happening she had me in her backyard, surrounded by breadfruit tress and lemongrass, "ready" to start melting things.

"You know, I'm only here to learn how to control this stuff, right? I don't want to actually *use* any of it."

She grinned at me again, eyes filled with delight as she saw what I assumed was my "potential." "You know why your boyfriend brought you here so early today?"

"Mrs. Peila..."

"Just call me Godmother, *Mana*."

"Oh, okay, well then, Godmother, um, he's not my boyfriend."

"Sure, sure, not yet but just you wait." she replied, waggling a finger at me. "An old woman knows."

I sighed, amused, shaking my head. "Oh goodness."

"Say 'oye nani,' that's how we say that around here. Now, Alex brought you here early, because now is the time when our power is strongest. At sunrise." She stretched a hand to the sky, gesturing at what was turning out to be a breathtaking beginning to the day. I looked where her hand was to see the great expanse of pink and orange streaked by clouds, with a nice, round sun glowing warmly on us and greeting the day. "Our power comes from the sun, *Mana*." She beamed at me again.

"Really?" I replied.

"Of course! Our people have always drawn strength from the sun's rays. They warm our souls, strengthen us from the inside out, and are the source of our gifts." I scrunched my eyebrows at her.

"You mean, there are multiple kinds of gifts?"

"Yes, *Mana*, yes," she replied, shaking her head. "There are gifts of growing plants, wielding wood, stone, and other natural elements, electricity, and some..." she paused, smiling to herself, "mind reading and control." She lost me there.

"Um, what does mind reading have to do with the earth and heat and stuff?" She put a hand on my heart. I felt her warm hand against my chest and soft heat began spreading through my body. She closed her eyes, breathing in deeply.

"I sense the electric currents running through your body, Mana, and I can read the impulses as well as change or control them. Some would probably call me a learner of the mind, but it is truly the gift to understand the heat within." She lifted her hand from me then, pausing to let me take it all in.

"Well then," I asked. "Which gift do I have?" I thought back to my fiasco the previous week and the now broken kitchen table. "Was it, uh, wood destroying or something?" She smirked at me, and her eyes then filled with wonder.

"*Mana*, I can see that you have the most powerful gift our people possess." I blinked at her, so she just continued, but this time grasped both of my hands in her own, cupping them together. "It is the gift of royalty. Only the royal line had this gift. They possessed the purest connection to the sun itself, which allowed them access to all gifts. We call you *Rose Wielders*, because the layers to your gift are as many as a rose. You can even direct the heat within a person's body to heal itself." My eyes widened as I thought of the man I had healed just days before. But suddenly, I found myself feeling confused. My father found my mother on the streets of the island and took her in as a charity case. We were not of noble blood by any stretch. But before I could respond she shushed me.

"Don't ask questions, *Mana*. Just feel the power within you, and don't hold it back." She closed her eyes and held my hands, so I did the same. Within a few moments, something warm and strong welled into my chest and then spread to my arms. Soon, my hands were glowing with heat in hers. It was steady and it was still. We just sat there, concentrating on me feeling my power intentionally for the first time since I was ten years old. Tears began to sting my face as I began to recall pieces of myself that I had held down for so long. Finally, I let my power subside.

We both opened our eyes then, and Peila, with a small smile and nod just replied, "Good. You probably won't be needing those oils or umbrellas anymore, you know." At this, she enveloped me in a bear hug, pressing me against herself. I felt another tear sting my cheek in that moment, and was surprised at myself. Unbeknownst to me, I think there was something inside of me that I was finally ready to explore.

It was time to unleash... me.

14

Roots

The following few weeks became something of a whirl-wind as I began to train under Peila. After really feeling my power for the first time like that, it just felt like something was awake inside of me. And... I couldn't help it, but I didn't want it to go back to sleep.

"So," I began one particularly sunny July afternoon, "How did Melindans get their powers again?" Peila and I were perched at the top of a mini hill, about a mile's walk from their home. It was the perfect training ground, complete with a cleared ground, multiple plants and all kinds of fruit trees for me to manipulate their energy, and a breathtaking view of the whole island. Most importantly, there was a direct view of the daily sunrise. You could almost feel the energy of the place watching you, beckoning you on to keep developing your skills.

"Keep punching!" she replied. I rolled my eyes and went back to my task of curling my fist to a tree. I was learning how to melt my way through wood today. Little Arabellasized knuckle marks were on the tree, glowing red with my gift and nicely singed around the edges. With each hit, I was learning how to concentrate my heat into just my knuckles, and meld its fibers further and further, until hopefully, the tree would fall.

"Godmother," I said, pausing again.

"Don't talk, just work!"

"But—"

"No!" She snapped. "A good Wielder knows how to do two tasks. Either speak and work or just work!" I nodded, taking a deep breath and furrowing my eyebrows determinedly, and wiping some sweat from my forehead before continuing.

"So," I managed through punches. "Tell me... where..." Deep breaths. "They... get their powers."

"Good, *Mana*," she said smiling. "Keep your back straight!" She directed, giving a good whack to my lower back. "Strong posture now! Well done. Now..." she said pausing to fold her arms and look at me thoughtfully. "How much do you know of our people?"

Punch, punch. Wipe sweat. "Not much." Breath. Punch!

"Good, *Mana*, good!"

"I just know that they were conquered, that's all really... Everything I've learned just always starts with them already defeated." I added the last part painfully, realizing I knew practically nothing of their beginnings.

"There's no shame here, Arabella. You are not to blame for this." I looked at her with a half-smile. "Okay, take a break," she said decidedly, patting a strong hand on my shoulder.

"Thank you," I answered breathlessly. She motioned for us to sit under a nearby tamarind tree with a beautiful bench, carved by Rupert himself. Then she handed me a tall, cool drink of muebe, smiling as she did so. Gratefully, I accepted the drink as I always did after a good day of training. Its refreshing sweetness was a great welcome to my system.

"Now," she began, taking a sip of her own thoughtfully, "the story of *our* people," she said, emphasizing the "our" part and raising an eyebrow at me. It was always so hard for me to claim a people I knew nothing about, and especially since all I knew of them... us, was destruction and defeat.

"Our people were once strong, Mana," she said, nodding her head slowly. "We had power, prestige, and wealth." She looked at me, pleased by the surprise on my face. "In fact, we ruled the entire southern hemisphere of this world. Our connection to the sun was quite strong then, and this made us virtually unstoppable."

"Is this where our powers stemmed from?"

She nodded again. "We have always had our powers from the sun. It is said that when the Creator made our people, he gave us a special connection to it, so much so that even our very skin drinks it in, darkening and deepening our great love for one another. What weakened and even burned other peoples only made us stronger still, and this is what the Promynthians were threatened by us."

"So when we came to conquer you, it was not in strength, but in weakness?"

"When the Promynthians came to our lands, it was in great fear. They came to weaken us before we weakened them. Their actions were an act of war."

I was confused. "But if they... we were so great, then how could they have conquered us?"

"They gained allies from the neighboring lands. They spread fear of us throughout the other nations, so together they were able to subdue us. It is not that all nations hate us, but rather that they fear us." I was shocked. Taking this in was incredible as well as somewhat crazy. I couldn't believe that people actually feared the Melindans at some point.

"And what about now? How do they see us now?" I asked.

"What do you think?" She grinned. "Of course they are still afraid. This is why they mistreat us and even have made our wielding illegal and like a myth now. If only our people could remember from whence we came, we could be strong enough to break the yoke of our oppressors." I looked down, taking it all in, feeling anger and hope welling up inside me all at once.

"I am in charge of strengthening this city. But if the people have forgotten who they are, how can they be empowered again?" I shook my head, heat welling in my fists now. "Who will remind them?"

She paused, flashing a smile, looking from my hands to my eyes. "We shall see."

As our apprenticeship stretched on, Alex, Crystal and I spent considerably more and more time with Peila and Rupert. For training, I started going early in the morning between six and nine in-the-morning if you can believe it. You get almost peak performance at that time, and no project or class would be in the way either. I guess even I could wake up for something as life-giving as wielding. Peila took time to train me practically every day.

In only a month, she had me moving from wood melding to stone melding, which I am hoping was altruistic of her, although I did find myself doing a lot of yard work that week...

Anyway, after that she moved me to starting to grow some fruit, which was pretty interesting. I guess I never thought about moving the electric currents through leaves and such, but it definitely made for some delicious tarts from the mango trees I grew overnight. And of course there was the classic of making good, old-fashioned fire to heat the stove, which made the curry stew cook even faster. But, there was still one thing she hadn't taught me yet.

"Mana," I asked her as we gardened one morning and I bade little lilies to start growing. She turned to face me, giving me her attention. "When will you teach me to read the mind?" She rolled her eyes, with amusement playing across her face now. "What?" I probed. "What did I say?"

"That is the one thing I cannot teach you, Arabella." I furrowed my eyebrows.

"I can learn!" I replied indignantly. She put a loving hand on my shoulder.

"No, *Mana.* This is not teachable, it is something that must come to you."

"And how am I supposed to know when it's there?"

She shook her head at me, but then looked up at me very gravely. "Arabella, reading the mind is no small feat. The way our gifts work is that we combine our energies with that of the thing that we wield. In order to wield a mind, we must allow our energy to become intertwined with the other without losing ourselves." She said the last part quietly. "Otherwise, it is you who will be controlled."

I nodded slowly, understanding somewhat but still feeling very confused. Looking at my blank face, she added, "You will know when the time is right. You will have to be in *exces-*

sive danger to do it for the first time. After that, you should be able to train yourself to read and influence others at any time."

I took a deep breath, taking in every word. But then I pursed my lips. How in the world would I get in a life-threatening situation like that?

15

Saturday

A few days later, Peila and Rupert started getting excited, because, "Well, it's one of the most important times of year!" I nodded obediently to Godmother, even though I was very confused.

"Tell us more about it, Godmother, please!" Crystal asked excitedly, jumping up and down, her bouncing curls following her. Today was Saturday, so Crys, Alex and I all had a day off and naturally made our way over here.

Peila smiled in response. "Of course I will! But not with you all sitting there all hungry like that!" She winked at us. Alex grinned happily (obviously). He always loved her good food.

Once we were surrounded by sufficiently piled bowls of salt fish, peppers and rice, she began her story. "So, some of you already know about the annual dance of our people." She turned to Alex, who was beaming. I squinted my eyes at him. *Why did he have to know everything?* "And," she continued, raising her eyebrows at me and snatching back my attention from my envy, "this year, due to Arabella's great work at the Dome of Walabe, they are inviting you three as their special guests of honor." My eyebrows raised in amazement. This sounded pretty cool for the most part, well, except for the dancing part. *But at least I won't have to—* "Dance is naturally a part of the whole thing," she completed my thoughts. I hated when she did that. "And so you'll all be expected to join in the festivities!" she said, clapping matter-of-factly. I shot a nervous glance to Crystal, but she was of no help at all. Instead, she was bouncing excitedly in her seat, grinning from ear to ear.

"I LOVE DANCING!" she squealed.

"You don't say," I replied sarcastically, squinting at her too. These "friends" of mine were just plain traitors today.

"It's okay, Bella," Alex said. "You won't have to do this alone." He nodded to Crystal. "We'll be right there with you the whole time." I rolled my eyes and shook my head. But, then, I thought again for a moment, knowing he was right. I probably owed it to them to show up, since I was invited.

I shut my eyes before taking a deep breath. "*Oye nani!*" I exclaimed, finally throwing up my hands. "You guys win. I'll go." They all cheered, pleased with their effective peer- pressuring tactics. "But," I added, shocking them all, "I'm only dancing *one time.*"

Peila shrugged her shoulders, completely unfazed. "We'll see if you can rip yourself away from the crowd, but you can certainly try!"

After spending time at the island, I headed over to the Dome of Walabe. I had asked August to meet me there, since he wanted to go on a date today. Godmother was sweet and had fashioned me some lace gloves for my date. She said a material wielder had given her the silk threads for it. I wore them proudly, hoping August would like them too.

I made it to the Dome just in time, because he was arriving by coach right as I rode up. He waved to me from the open window. I smiled back. "Arabella!" he exclaimed, hugging me close once he was out of his ride. I held him close. He was so sweet and warm, and I just loved savoring every moment with him.

"How was the ride?" I asked, as we stopped hugging but still held hands.

"Really good, pretty fast," he replied. "Hey, want to eat on the patio tonight?"

"Sure," I agreed, shrugging my shoulders.

For the meal, we had bread rolls, spiced lamb, jelly syrup and mixed greenery. It was so romantic to be out under the stars with him like this. Although the candles we had set up were super sweet as well.

"Bella, how was it wielding today?"

"Oh, it was really cool."

"Did you learn anything new?"

I paused, remembering what Peila had said about being in danger. "Well, I did learn that I can probably learn how to read minds at some point."

"Seriously?"

"Yeah, it seems sort of hard, so I'm not worrying about it right now," I replied shrugging.

"No, no, there's something you aren't telling me."

I pursed my lips. Of course he knew. "Okay, okay. So when

I read minds, I have to be careful, because otherwise, I'll be put under the control of whoever's mind I'm trying to read."

He blinked a few times. "Well that seems intense."

"It is, silly!" I exclaimed laughing and nudging him. "See? This is why power isn't all it's cracked up to be."

"Well," he replied, "I think it just depends on who's in charge."

"That's fair," I said, smiling. That's when he took my hand and had me stand up with him. Then he wrapped his hands around my waist, so I put mine around his neck, naturally.

"Bella, are you afraid of having all that power?" he whispered.

"You know I am," I said softly.

"Well, what if you didn't have to wield it all alone?"

I scrunched my eyebrows. "What do you mean?"

"I promise to be by your side as you figure this whole power thing out, okay? I won't leave you." My stomach melted with butterflies as I smiled at him. We were just swaying back and forth to music in our minds.

"You promise?" I whispered.

"I'll prove it," he whispered back. That's when he bent down and pressed his lips against mine to kiss me. I totally melted then.

16

Dance

Feeling all dreamy and giddy about boys has its perks. The downsides are that we forget about things we've promised to do. Things that involve public embarrassment and shame, such as through dancing. Which brings me to the night of the Melindan dance party, which snuck up on me rudely. I found myself on the stage at the beginning of the festivities of the night. I wasn't really nervous of speaking, because I actually enjoyed public speaking. I actually looked forward to addressing these people, as I had really gotten to learn so much about them this summer, and just wanted so badly to thank them for that opportunity. (It was the dancing.)

I started my speech, hopeful that I could somehow escape. "People of Melinda," I began in a loud voice. I looked out over the vast expanse of black faces staring back at me with fire in their eyes. It was an unmistakable fire, the flame of hope that lit them. They looked at me and saw themselves. They saw that through me, they had a voice. And I felt determined to be so for them. I strained my throat to make sure my message could reach those in the back row. "I wanted to say that I am so grateful for the opportunity to speak to you all." A few voices called my name gleefully. I appreciated the support, acknowledging them with a smile, and continued on. "This has truly been the summer of a lifetime, and I have enjoyed learning so much about my own people through this apprenticeship!"

The crowd let out a cheer, filling me with adrenaline. I breathed in deeply. "What happened to you the day at Walabe was completely wrong and unjust. I am sorry that the guards there did not protect you more." A sobering silence filled the air. "Even though I too felt helpless that day, the truth is that there was a power inside of me that was made to protect you." I looked down at my hands, the ones I had shunned for so long. Courageously, I held them out in front of me, allowing them to sparkle for all to see. "What I possess inside belongs to all of us, and it is our collective spirit that will help us to thrive. Each of you has a gift that makes us stronger together. I vow to use mine to protect you." I looked out at the crowd now, at each and every one of those resilient faces. "That day in Walabe, our hearts were lit aflame together, and I am determined to be the voice you need once I am crowned your princess."

Widespread cheering followed this as well as some applause. "I will be your representative in the royal palaces. I will show the courts what strengths we possess, what gifts we have. We do not deserve to be shut out from our land, and cornered to an island." My voice felt stronger now, so I raised it, filled with belief from my core outward. "Promynthia is a land made of many people, and is as much an idea and an experiment in the human spirit, as it is a nation state. As my father has always said, unity and mercy are our strength. Let us be unified, then, with our sisters and brothers and make this a greater Promynthia for *all* of us. Let's be truly Promynthian at heart!"

I shouted this last line, and lifted my hands in the air, throwing my head back and shooting fireworks into the air. I left one hand spread wide in the air, showing my solidarity and connectedness with all of my people. Many across the expanse of the crowd followed suit, and soon we had many waving their arms in the air, sparkling with their own colored light, in agreement with my message. They shouted back at me with greater pride and energy than I have ever heard, "Promynthian at HEART!!" Cheers filled the entire area where we stood, and music began playing, drowning out any semblance of silence.

A young woman came onto the wooden stage and invited the people to sing with her. This is when she pulled out a mandolin and began to strum it sweetly. Then she lifted up her soft yet powerful voice, and with it, the rest of the crowd was also lifted up. Together, they sang and their collective sound swelled high into the palm trees and night sky above. I scurried off the stage to find Crystal, but she had apparently gone off to be in the midst of the crowd to meet people. All I found was Alex where I last left her. We stood there for a moment, taking in the music and seeing the people singing and swaying along, many keeping their hands in the air.

Then Alex read my thoughts and answered them. "This is the original Melindan anthem," he whispered to me.

"It's... beautiful," I whispered back.

"Land that I love, land of my heart, people who are a work of art," he translated. "Sing with me now, twirl and dance, people I love, Melinda advance!" I smiled at him. He was such a nerd for knowing this language so well.

Suddenly, the elder of the island, Great Bufunde was beckoning me to come back onto the humble stage. "Princess!" he shouted, smiling from ear to ear. I walked back up and he enveloped me in the warmest of hugs. The crowd cheered again. He continued with, "We, the people of Melinda, ask you to appear at our annual festival, in one fortnight, as a thank you for your riveting words and royal support throughout your apprenticeship."

"Thank you, Great Bufunde," I said, curtsying to him.

"This is excellent, Princess! And to ready you for this occasion, we will now celebrate with a preliminary victory dance!" My eyes widened with shock. Before I could protest, he signaled the band with a loud clap, and musicians appeared from the opposite end of the stage with mandolins, drums, and flutes and began to play. That's when the entire crowd broke out *dancing*!

Nerves lurched into my stomach, and I stood there, frozen and wide-eyed. I wasn't necessarily that great of a dancer, and I didn't want to embarrass myself in front of these beautiful people. Clearly they knew what they were doing, as they began twirling and twisting into the night against the dark background lit by multiple lamps surrounding the dance floor. But before I could find a way to slowly crawl back off the stage, I felt someone's presence right next to me.

"Alex, thank goodness!" I said quickly. "You've got to help me find a way out of here!"

"The only way out is through, Bella."

I glared at him. "I am *not* dancing, Alexander." The two of us looked out at Crystal, twirling happily and being passed from person to person. I shook my head thinking about how much fun she was probably having. Why couldn't I be… less me, and more like her? I mean, at least in convenient times like this?

I shook my head and turned back to him, folding my arms across my chest. He looked me up and down and just chuckled. "You know it will build your trust with them, right?" I glared at him. "Plus, you promised Godmother," he whispered smugly.

My heart sank a little. I had really hoped everyone had forgotten about that by now. "*Oye nani,*" I admitted, sighing. Finally I conceded. "Fine, but just *one* dance," I agreed, holding up my finger so it was clear how little I would be joining in that night.

"I'll take it," he said shrugging, and then slowly held my hand with his left, while placing his right hand behind my left shoulder. "Is this okay?" He asked, his voice getting a little shaky. (Um, why was his voice shaking?)

"Yeah, sure," I replied, looking slightly puzzled now.

"Okay, just… follow my lead," he said, after taking a deep breath. *Was that sweat I saw forming on his forehead?* Just as he did so, the music went from a super-fast song to a much slower one. Yep, this was just what I needed.

"Step to the back," he tried instructing me. But he was faster than me and quickly stepped on my foot.

"Ouch!" I whined dramatically, but then giggled. This was

going to be interesting. Alex didn't seem to think it was so funny though.

"I'm so sorry, Princess! Um, Arabella!" I realized that he was probably super nervous. Being the generous soul I am, I decided to rescue him.

Grasping his arms with my own, I stopped him from looking down with horror at my foot. "Alex. Alex! It's okay." I said, staring intently at him, hoping to calm him down. "We're just not great dancers, and that's okay. Let's just have fun, okay?"

"You're right," he agreed nodding. And I thought *I* was the nervous one! *What did he even have to be nervous about?*

"Okay," he began again, with some renewed confidence. "You step back when I step forward, see?" he tried again, this time much more slowly. "And then we step to the side like that, and I twirl you around once in a while."

I smiled as we tried practicing the moves. "Oh, I get it! Hey, we're actually doing great, Alex. You're a good teacher!" He grinned in return, and then spun me around three times. After that, a faster song came on.

"Want me to find you a new partner?" he offered.

I raised an eyebrow. "And dance with strangers? Thanks but that's a definite no!" We both laughed.

"Oh well, I guess it's you and me then," he replied, shrugging his shoulders.

"Okay, yeah, what's this one?" I replied excitedly. Before I knew it, we were dancing together for at least an hour. Seriously, Alex was such a good teacher. He was so reassuring, I didn't feel like I had to impress him or like I was two steps (Ha, see what I did there?) from making a big mistake! I don't think I'd ever want another dancing partner. After the seventh song in a row we were both exhausted, not just from dancing but probably from the emotion of the whole day. Wearily, I looked out to see if I could find Crystal anywhere. It didn't take long to find her blond curls gleefully twirling from one dark suitor to another. I guess her dream was coming true. Chuckling to myself, I shook my head at her. *How could one person possibly have so much energy?* Alex and I both knew Peila and Rupert would not leave without her, so we decided to head back to the palace early. As soon as my head hit the pillow, I drifted right asleep.

17

⧂

Proposal

After that night, I found myself really understanding Alex better. Sure he was a little awkward, but he was also so sweet and patient. I appreciated his weird obsession with Melindan culture, even if it did put me to shame sometimes. I was reflecting on this at dinner when August touched my arm.

"Bella, want to go for a walk?"

I flashed a smile at him and squeezed his hand. I felt excited and nervous. I guess that's how you feel when you really *really* like someone. "Sure," I replied. Soon, we found ourselves arm in arm and headed down a walking trail that wrapped around the woods that flanked the Dome.

"And how are you, Bella?" he asked in his usual way. It was slowly becoming evening, but not without a beautiful sunset in view.

"I'm good— I've been having a lot of fun with Crystal lately."

"Yes, she is quite the cousin, isn't she?" he chuckled.

"Yes. Quite," I responded, smiling. "She told me… is it true that my uncle wanted you two together?" He rolled his eyes.

"Oh, *that*," he said, shaking his head.

"So," I said, chuckling to distract myself from the feeling of my stomach churning, "you don't have feelings for her?" he stopped walking, pausing and looking at me. I was hopelessly mesmerized.

"It could never work out between us, Arabella," he replied finally. "I—" he began, but stopped and walked ahead of me. I thought I detected a little flush in his cheeks. "I would want to be with someone else," he almost whispered. I felt myself dizzying, but shook it off, grabbing my ruffled skirt and running up next to him.

"Really?" I jested. But before I could continue questioning him, he beat me to it!

"And Alex?" he probed. I smirked, folding my arms.

"What about him?"

"Are you just friends?"

I laughed aloud. "Why does everyone ask me that?"

He shrugged. "Maybe because outside of me, you two spend so much time together?"

I gasped playfully. "What! Who is saying that?"

"I mean, people have seen you two laughing together, having fun and hanging out with Crystal together a lot. It raises questions."

I shook my head forcefully. "No, we just… we're just friends." I settled for confidently. But thinking about this made me wonder if there was something I was missing. Ignoring myself, though, I continued with August.

"Now, who, might I ask, is that lucky girl whom you want

to be with?" I asked. He smirked at me, and walked ahead again. I internally squealed before running after him again. Finally, we came to the end of the dirt road, with a clearing that looked over that whole area of the land, showing mountains and grasses further and further away. Beautiful daisies and wildflowers dotted the landscape tantalizingly. Gently, he reached out for my hands.

"That depends," he said gingerly, now kissing my hand. "That depends on if she will dine with me." I could have fainted from happiness. I flipped my hair, unable to control myself.

"Wait, when?"

"Tomorrow evening," he replied, now brighter red than I've seen him before. "At the Dome of Walabe. My father will join us."

"Well," I said, looking down at my feet, "That sounds special, I do hope she comes." He didn't break his gaze with me.

"I hope so too," he almost whispered. My heart beat faster now, and I stopped controlling myself inside, feeling the orange and purple rays of the sunset calling out to me.

"Ouch! Bella, your hands?" he exclaimed, letting go of me. I jumped back from him, holding out my arms, realizing that they were indeed sort of, well, steaming. "Oh my gosh, are you okay?" he continued.

"Yes, it's nothing! I feel fine!" I tried being casual and laughing it off.

"You're not going to fry me, are you?" He asked, grinning now. I chuckled again for good measure.

That night, I could hardly contain myself. I couldn't wait to tell Crystal the latest update. I poked her, giving her a dashing look and hoping she would read my mind. She rolled her eyes at me, chewing on a forkful of veggies. "What happened now?" she added, sighing. I nudged her with my elbow. She chuckled and then added "Ha ha, okay, what did you two talk about?"

I wrinkled my nose in excitement. "He wants me to meet him at the dome for dinner tomorrow again!"

"Just for dinner?" she said, pursing her lips.

"Crystal!" I said indignantly. She just raised her eyebrows at me in suspicion. "He's inviting me to dinner with his father this time!"

"He WHAT?!" she yelled, slamming the table with both hands and almost choking on her last piece of spinach. Everyone looked over at the two of us now. We looked back at them with wide eyes for at least 5 painful seconds before slowly rising and leaving the dinner table (but of course not without a few extra dinner rolls for good measure).

In the sleeping chamber we continued our conversation in hushed tones.

"Arabella, you do know what this means, right?" she asked me, eyes wide.

"Of course I do," I replied. "This means that August wants to spend more time with me and meet his family." She closed her eyes in frustration.

"No, Bella, it means that he's going to ask *for your hand,*" I looked at her then, taking in the statement and dropping to my knees.

"Um, what?"

She shook her head at me. "Bella, haven't your parents taught you *anything*?"

"I don't know," I replied, now getting into a fetal position on the floor trying to process her words.

She took a deep breath. "Well, that's what's happening, just so you know."

I tried to take in this whole scenario, just playing it through in my mind. The flowers, the walking, the flirting. It was wild to think that he liked me for *real*. Like, maybe even loved me. "Crystal, I'm suddenly so nervous," I said, shaking and chuckling a little too.

"Your parents will be there, you know."

"Where? How so?"

"They'll be at the dinner— it's a formal engagement, of course." It was all I could do not to pee my nightgown. After that, I couldn't really sleep. I was all mixed between excitement and something like dread. I guess sometimes this is how love feels? Why was I mixed between such strong emotions? As I flipped myself from the left to the right side, pulling my covers with me, the answer came into my head. *My parents.* I closed my eyes then, wishing that I didn't have to confront them tomorrow. No, talking to my parents was one thing. Talking to my mother? A different thing entirely. I had to get some advice. Finally, I determined to just ask Godmother what to do. Yawning, I tossed back to the other side, hoping for her words of wisdom to help me.

"He asked you WHAT?" she exclaimed, when I finished filling her in with what was going on between me and August. We were sitting in the garden in their backyard again. Slowly, it was nearing evening hours, and the sky was streaked with burnt orange streaks from the slowly waning sun.

"I know. I know! I guess it just all happened so fast!"

Peila just shook her head at me, chuckling. "And you love this boy?" I tried searching into myself, into every fiber of my nervous body to answer, but all I could think about was his brown hair, broad shoulders, and the kindness of his gestures, always a listening and supportive ear. I felt my face getting warm and tried hiding it with my hands. Peila just threw back her head laughing. "Well, I guess that answers that!" she said, slapping me on the knee in her glee.

I let out a nervous sigh in response. "I really can't hide much from you, can I, Godmother?"

She raised her brows. "Try to hide from me? A mind wielder? Ha!" Then she enveloped me in a hug and whispered to me, "I'm just a little disappointed that I didn't call things between you and Alex." She let go of me now. "But, if you truly love this August boy, then you must go to the dinner, even if you are unsure of yourself." I nodded in response.

"You're right," I replied, shrugging. "I guess it's just so scary to really be doing this in real life."

"This is true," she responded to me. But before she could add more, a rugged Rupert appeared from the village on the path leading to their home, carrying roses in a beautiful woven basket.

"For you, my Dears," he said, smiling and offered one to me before giving Peila the rest of the basket.

"Oh, you," Peila said, grinning and pulling him in for a quick kiss. I just sat there watching them.

"What are you looking at, *Mana*?" Rupert asked me, catching my longing stare. But before I could answer, he took it right out of my mind. "*Oye nani*, are you in love?" I shrugged my shoulders sheepishly. "Who is the boy?" he asked earnestly.

I looked up from my sweaty palms to his face. "You mean, you don't think it's Alex?"

"Of *course* not. No young woman goes after the *obvious* man in front of them— *that* would make too much sense," he said, eyeing Peila playfully. She gave him a deserving nudge with her basket, as I chuckled at the exposure.

"Are you really going to bring that up, *Mana*?" she asked in annoyance.

"Bring what up?" I felt excited now. "Wait, is this something about the story of how you two met?" Peila rolled her eyes. Rupert, attempting to persuade her, took her into his arms gently.

"Can't we tell the girl? She is like a daughter to us now." Peila pursed her lips, but was fighting back a smile. "Ah, Peila, my dear, I know that face!" Gently he kissed her on her forehead before earnestly pleading with his eyes again. "Please?"

Finally, she broke her resolve. "Okay, okay. But make sure to talk about yourself being crazy too, *Mana!*" He chuckled before turning to me.

"So, about 40 years ago, Pei and I met for the first time. I was working in the mines at that time and she was working with the young children— you know, reading their minds and helping their mothers know what they needed."

"She was a nurse?"

"Yes, very much so!"

"And a good one too," Peila chimed in. "All the children loved me, hmph!"

"One day, I got hurt while doing some chopping and my workmates rushed me to the hospital to fix my bleeding hand. The skin wielders did their surgery on me, using both medicine and secret wielding, and so I was healed. But before they let us leave the hospital, we speak to the mental nurses to make sure we're feeling okay."

"And that's how you met Peila?"

He turned, smiling at her. "Yes, as the Creator would have it, she was assigned to me that day. And immediately I felt a great spark between us."

"Hmph!" Peila interrupted, turning to me and folding her arms. "I have *no* idea what he's talking about."

"*Continuing on,*" he retorted, "I began to find reasons to come to the medicine house every day. Perhaps to bring more supplies, more stone from the mines, anything they needed. Well, anything to let me see Peila."

I sighed dreamily. "That's so beautiful!" I exclaimed. But then I felt confused. "Wait, how was she missing something?"

"Well," he said, turning to her again, "She thought I was just being a very good friend to her."

"*Puna wana,* is what we call them," she added. "A good friend, someone who you care for deeply but not in a romantic way."

"Ohhh," I nodded, catching on. "What a good word to know. So Alex is like my *'puna wana'*?"

"Unfortunately!" she replied with a chortle.

"Peila had strong feelings for another man, for a fellow nurse who rarely gave her any second thought."

"Why, Godmother!" I asked her. She tried to defend herself.

"It was the *adventure*, Mana." She exclaimed. "I just wanted to prove to him, to *myself*, that I was worth loving." She shook her head, shrugging her shoulders. "I guess I was so blinded by the chase, I never saw the goodness right in front of me." She said the last part softly, turning back to Rupert and holding his hand now. After a long pause, she added, "But, at least he didn't give up on me. No, he kept pursuing until I could accept that he was hopelessly in love with me for being... me."

The two of them standing there, loving each other, accepting each other in 40 years of marriage? That's literally all I wanted in the whole world.

18

Dinner

The following evening, I stepped down out of my coach, steadying myself with August's sure, steady hand, and beaming into his deep green eyes. My life was about to change forever, and I could feel it, warm as the hand I now touched. Arm in arm, we approached the Dome, ready to announce our commitment to one another. The only thing that made me hesitate was the thought of my parents on the other end of that opening hallway, waiting for me and to see the man I'd chosen as my beloved. Trying to shake away those thoughts, I took in a deep breath. I could do this with August by my side. Smiling, I turned to him and whispered, "I'm sorry my parents are going to be a lot for you!"

"And that's different from you *how*?" he replied. I chuckled, nudging him in the side.

"Hey! I'm cool," I defended.

Warmly, he squeezed my arm, which was locked firmly with his own, and grinned widely. "You're amazing, Bella." I grinned in response. He surely knew how to say the right words. Confidently, we entered his father's Dome, ready to face them together.

Since it was obviously a special night, I tried to dress up more than usual. Crystal certainly approved of my gown, a cream floor-length one with dramatic swooping layers and sleeves that draped around the sides of my shoulders. Peila had contributed again too, giving me a great gift for my hair, to add a Melindan touch— a garland of cream lilies from the garden we had wielded together. They matched perfectly with the dress, and I added white sparkles to my cheeks. I was thrilled with the final product. I appreciated August's outfit too. He looked the part of a perfect prince in his simple, black suit. We were like yin and yang, opposites to balance on another out. I couldn't wait to start our lives together.

We entered the Dome gracefully, and let the servants take our outer cloaks before heading into the dinner chamber. Already seated were his father and... my parents. They were sitting there sipping on drinks and appetizers, having quite the conversation. My mother was laughing gleefully and my father's face was red with amusement as well. I guess they were getting along!

When they saw us enter, their conversation immediately stopped, and they looked to us radiantly. We all stood there for a moment, taking in one another's presence. My father broke the silence by standing gleefully and walking over to me. "Arabella, my Darling!" he exclaimed, coming and wrapping me in his arms. I buried my face in his chest, smiling, and let him envelop me completely. I had forgotten how much I missed his big, safe embrace. After a long moment we parted, but he did not let his hands leave my shoulders. "Dear, you look so beautiful tonight!"

"Thank you, Father." I said gleefully. Mother did not bother to stand, but she did look like she was beaming. Happily, she locked eyes with me, obviously proud that I had met her "secret" request to find myself a match here.

"Yes, Dear," she added to Father's words, "you look just *stunning*." I curtsied for her, hoping it was enough to keep her impressed. She tugged a little on her high dark turtleneck, obviously thinking to herself how to transition to The Boy. Her face was not hard to read as she looked him over quickly, her mind clearly racing with questions. And so she began. "Please introduce us to your... friend." We took that as our cue, and glanced nervously at one another before nodding to each other for reassurance. August read my mind and pulled out a seat for me opposite his father, before seating himself directly in front of my parents. He was making some bold moves tonight.

"This," I started, holding onto his hand for support, "is August Frederick IX. He has been my partner for the duration of this apprenticeship, and we have been working together on the province of Melinda." My mother nodded, approving so far, so I continued. "But, he's more than just a partner now, Your Majesty."

"That's wonderful to hear, Dear!" Father said with a laugh, throwing his head back. "This is what we like to hear!" Mother was still squinting at August, obviously deciding whether to accept him or to behead him. However, Father now turned his full attention to August. "Tell me, Son, what fancies you about my daughter?"

August glanced at me excitedly before answering. Clearly this must have been the moment he had been preparing for! "Your Majesty," he started, but cleared his throat from nerves. His confidence seemed to wane now, so he just turned his gaze fully towards me. "I have never met a more beautiful and intelligent woman than Arabella Bysentor, and I cannot imagine living my life without her with me."

My father nodded approvingly. "Yes, Son, that's exactly how I felt about her mother."

Mother didn't seem too phased by the comment, though. Boldly, she chimed in, too. "And what of her lineage? How do you feel that she is half-Melindan? Is this something you can accept?" My eyes widened, and I felt my cheeks starting to get warm. Was she really going to bring this up *now*? Even though it was the hippo in the room, somehow I still did not feel comfortable talking about differences like that in his presence. I wanted to draw as much attention away from that as possible.

But contrary to my fears, August just kept looking at me and grinning, though he was responding to her question. "I truly wouldn't want to have things any other way." Happiness stirred in my head and made me feel dizzy. *Was I flying? Did I really just hear him say those words, accepting me as a Melindan in front of his own father?*

The duration of the meal did not feel long, as we continued conversing in that way. My parents questioning August, his father just nodding intently, and August talking for the both of us. As the three of them continued, I would steal glances at his father. He looked similar to his son, except his hair was much darker in color, except for the sides, which had distinct streaks of silver mixed in with the black. Likewise, his frame, as tall as his son's but much thinner and more hunched, made him look something like a lizard rather than the youthful vibrant son I would marry. I guess August just got his good looks from his mother. Sometimes he would catch me stealing glances at him and he would just nod slowly. It seemed he knew I was just trying to take in his appearance, as if he knew his odd appearance confused many.

As soon as we had all finished, we went out to the patio to enjoy the stars and the beautiful night air. It was a peaceful evening, with dark, warm air, and not a cloud in sight. The servants had made the decorations dreamy to perfection, with many candles and draping tablecloths and curtains lining the usually bare stone walls. As we all stood there taking it in, August's father chuckled. "We're glad you like the look. I guess things might be changing a bit more around here with a more feminine touch!" He clapped his hands firmly to his son's shoulders, clearly proud of the great match we would be. My heart welled with hope looking at the sight, my dear August beaming with my father and my parents wrapped arm in arm looking out over the night sky— finally, I was doing something my family would all be proud of. But apparently it wasn't over yet.

August removed himself from his father, giving him a playful wink, before turning to me determinedly. "Arabella?" he asked.

"Yes?" I replied, breathy but elated.

He took my hand in his own. "Will you accompany me to our garden?"

"Naturally," I replied, smiling. He led me away from the

group then, and I willfully followed, not able to contain my giggling. In a few minutes, we were surrounded by shrubbery and flowers. But, he led me deeper in, to a bench which was lit with more candles surrounding it and more cream curtains in the tree above it.

"Oh, August!" I exclaimed then, tears beginning to well in my eyes. I had never had anyone do something so beautiful and thoughtful for me like this. He grinned, not responding, but led me to sit and knelt down on one knee beside me, never letting go of my hand. (Thank goodness he didn't or I might have fainted from happiness.)

"Arabella?" he tried to begin, but then cleared his throat, to start again. "Arabella, I know this apprenticeship has been only three months, but in that time I have come to know you as a partner and a princess, and I hope to know you more than this." I breathed in deeply, taking in every word. "Arabella, you are the most beautiful woman I have ever met, and I must ask you, will you be my bride?"

More tears filled my eyes, and I shut them trying to drown them out. Why did I feel like I didn't deserve such special treatment? What was wrong with me? August, noticing my pausing, looked concerned. "Is everything alright?"

Quickly I shook it away. It was just fear and was getting in the way of this special moment. I opened my eyes, letting the tears stream down. "Yes, nothing could be better, August! Yes, I accept!" I managed breathily. I had really hoped that this would be more majestic, but I guess this was all I could muster in the moment. Too bad for smooth romance.

But he didn't seem to mind. Chuckling, he stood and pulled me up to stand with him, wrapping me in his arms. I closed my eyes, shaking with nerves, but his warmth made me feel calm.

"Maybe this will help?" he suggested, lifting my chin to his face. Then, he bent down and kissed me. I melted again and all of my fear went away. In that moment, I knew this was the man I was going to marry, and I knew we would be stronger together.

19

Plans

I don't think I'll ever forget that magical night, nor the great warmth that filled my soul by seeing my parents and August's dad coming together in such an incredible and joyous way. Every moment was worth it, especially the time in the garden. I was a bride-to-be now, and so *floored* by that very thought.

When I finally made it home that evening, Crystal was there, waiting in my bed for all of the details. I giggled, telling her everything and shedding a few more tears. She hugged me again and again telling me how proud she was of me and how beautiful of a bride I would be. I let her sleep in my bed that night, especially after us talking until three in the morning.

The following day was not so magical and merciful though. Even though night brought me life, I had to pay for it in the morning. Today, August and I had a long day ahead of us of meeting with the prime minister of a neighboring province, to try to gain more monetary support for our province for the final task of our apprenticeship. It would be the first of many official adventures together, and I felt so happy to have him by my side.

As we rode along in the bumpy carriage, he reached over and squeezed my hand. "It's going to be a great day," he said, smiling at me, and planted a quick kiss for extra measure.

"Thanks," I replied softly.

"Although," he said, eyeing me nervously, "I think it could help if you would pull your hair back."

I scrunched my eyebrows. "What do you mean?" I cocked my head towards him, curls bouncing to one side.

He shook his head. "Don't take offense, Bella. It's just that the prime minister is sort of... old fashioned, that's all."

"And?"

"And..." he said, leaning over and beginning to pull my hair into a bun, "so it could be good for you to put it back," he said, chuckling.

I rolled my eyes at him. "You, always with the rules," I said, shaking my head. "Let me do this, you know you couldn't anyway." We laughed together as I pulled it into a bun.

Soon enough, we had reached the palace, and in practically no time, were sitting to tea with the prime minister, Hunterson. He was a short man, probably in his 80s, and wore a very large hat. His robes seemed to weigh his small body to the ground. And he was nearly blind. That's when we began to negotiate funds. As the men spoke, I sipped my cinnamon tea quietly.

"And so, Minister Hunterson," August explained, "the state of the people is quite unbearably sad. And this is why we are coming to you for extra... support."

Hunterson clicked his tongue slowly. "These... commoners

always want money, but without any work on their part." He shook his head.

"My dear Sir," August continued, "it is imperative that these people receive these enrichments. Furthermore, the people themselves are ignorant of what to do with the resources. And have no fear, Sir. The money will not go to the Melindanpeople themselves, but to the Grand Duke of Walabe, my father, who will ensure that it goes to its proper place." I raised an eyebrow at him.

Minister Hunterson nodded his head slowly. "Very well," he agreed, "I do trust your father greatly. He will know what to do better than any Melindan."

I swallowed hard. "Sir, if I might add," I began, clearing my throat. August looked at me with wide green eyes. "Perhaps... um, perhaps we can implement a program to empower the people themselves in areas of enterprise and education. I am sure that they can learn whatever skills as well as any of our Promynthian people."

He chuckled. "Mellos can't learn a thing." I bristled. "But you will never understand their ignorance," he continued, with a wave of his hand. Looking me up and down he added, "I can see you are hardly 'Melindan' yourself." He chuckled.

I stared at him intently, feeling my fists curling and thinking of the lively, beautiful city I had grown to love. "Sir, if I might add, the people do have very great gifts as wielders which would be indispensable to the kingdom were we to utilize them."

He nearly choked on his vanilla cake. "Wha—!" But he couldn't finish his thought because he was sputtering and coughing up the cake.

"Sir!" August exclaimed, coming up next to him and patting his back firmly.

"Yes, I am fine," he stated a little after containing himself. To me he said, "Girl, those demons can't write their own name, let alone use some powers!"

"But, Sir!" I pushed back.

"No, you obviously don't know your history, girl," he chuckled. To August, he added, "Son, take care of her now, and make sure she doesn't get into any trouble." I squinted at him, wondering what he meant, but was silent. The two of them carried on their conversation of what they were to do with my people.

On the carriage ride back to the Dome, August and I were mostly silent. After several minutes, I asked, "August, are you okay?"

He continued staring out the window, but said, "Yes, I'm fine." After another minute of silence he added, "But Bella, you really took my chance to run a good bargain and now, we won't receive the money because you wanted to prove that those people can do something."

"Well, can't we?" I asked, frustration welling in my chest.

"No," he said shortly. "You know, you are not one of them, Bella." He waggled a finger at me. "You can't save the Melindans from themselves. We all know they got there by their own choices." I didn't respond to him, and instead just looked out my side of the coach. His lack of faith in my people hurt me to my core. I didn't feel I could respond.

I could tell he was staring at me, waiting for my response. Waiting for him to apologize, I just kept silent. Finally, he reached over and hugged me.

"Bella," he said softly, flashing those big green eyes at me. "I'm sorry." I rolled my eyes at him, but he went ahead and kissed my forehead.

"What will I do with you, August?" I asked him, finally nestling safe in his arms.

"Come to the Dome Ball with me."

"Of course! Who else would I go with?" I laughed softly as he tucked my flyaways behind my ear. At that moment I realized it was the same night as the Melindan festival. *How had I forgotten?* I assured myself Alex and Crys would have a plan. We passed a few more peaceful, yet bumpy moments in silence.

20

Ball

Carefully, I applied blue, iridescent powder to my eyelids to make them sparkle brightly. I figured it would be a nice touch to add to my gown, a shimmery mess of ocean blue itself. Hopefully my unruly curls would stay in their place tonight. Unfortunately, I highly doubted that. Eventually, I gave in and just straightened it, before pulling it up.

With another deep breath, I began applying pink color to my lips. This makeup would be the most colored part of me tonight. Since it was a special occasion, I decided to double up on powder. *Traditional,* I thought to myself. Lightly tapping my brush against the powder box and watching the excess particles float to the basin, I wondered to myself if August would approve.

"Hey, you," a male voice at my chamber door called. A head peered inside and locked eyes with mine.

"Alex," I smiled warmly. Behind him, I could see Crystal peering over his shoulder.

"I can't wait for the festival tonight!" she said excitedly, now pushing Alex aside to hug me. They had figured out that we could always leave the ball early and head over there. "And, sweetheart, you look so beautiful!" she exclaimed. I beamed at her. But then her eyebrows scrunched as she touched my cheek and some white leapt to her fingers. "Wait, why are you wearing so much powder tonight?"

"Yeah, you look sort of... dead, Bella," Alex added, tilting his head to the side. Crystal and I glared at him. He looked panicked.

Rolling our eyes, we returned to our conversation. "I just..." I began to explain. "I'm trying out a more traditional look. I just want to look good for August tonight, that's all. "

She squinted her eyes at me. "By becoming *pale*?"

"Crystal, you don't understand," I began, feeling impatient and beginning to raise my voice. "Wherever you go, you always look right! Not me. I have to find ways to try to look like you just to be taken seriously around here!"

She grew very quiet. "I'm sorry, Bella," she replied. "I didn't think about what I was saying and how it was affecting you. I just want you to feel like you can be yourself."

"Well, in a perfect world we could all do that. Everyone would be loved just the way they are, whether they looked like me or you. But clearly that's not the world we live in!" I said.

She looked down. "I just hope August sees you the right way." Now I grew quiet. I hoped so too. To break the silence, we started walking over to the ballroom. That's when I looked twice at Alex, not completely believing what I was seeing.

"You clean up very well," I said, surprised.

"Ah," he said, grinning smugly. "What can I say? When you've got a good base to work with..."

"Whatever," I said, rolling my eyes. Crystal just laughed loudly.

"Okay, okay," he said, chuckling, "just don't forget to meet up at the stable at midnight, alright?" Crystal and I nodded gleefully.

"And Bella?" Crystal said to me. "Remember that every relationship has bumps, and it's okay not to be perfect all the time."

I half-smiled at her. "Thanks, girl."

By this point, we had made it right to the entrance of the grand ballroom. The light from inside it was almost blinding. It was so beautifully decorated inside, and my jaw was slowly dropping. "Princess," August said, bowing to me and holding out his arm. He had approached at that moment. Alex bowed, taking Crystal by the arm, and they were gone. But just before they left, Crystal gave me a much needed wink as if to say, *you've got this!* Smiling at her, I swallowed hard and then turned to August, curtsying.

"Where have you been?" he asked.

"I was just getting ready," I replied.

"Oh, okay," he replied. "I was really looking all over for you. Remember, we had planned to take a stroll just before the evening?" My cheeks grew warm.

"We did? Oh gosh, I'm so sorry August. I really completely forgot!"

"I gathered as much," he chuckled, nudging me softly.

"No, it's not funny, I really wanted tonight to be perfect!" He put a reassuring hand on my shoulder.

"It's totally okay, Arabella. You know, you're so cute when you're frazzled?" I smirked at him. "Come on, let's have fun," he continued. I accepted his arm and together we entered the shimmering room. I looked up at him again slowly with a light smile.

"Can we just enjoy tonight?" I said, gingerly. This past week was just so exhausting, between getting engaged, talking to the godparents and now especially with that weird interaction at the new Dome. All I wanted was a positive night. "I know I've sort of messed up recently and I—" But he interrupted me by kissing my gloved hand.

"Don't worry about yesterday. Let's make sure tonight is one you'll never forget." I beamed gratefully at him.

The ballroom was nothing short of spectacular. The light brown wooden floors were impeccably shiny, and the ceiling seemed to go higher and higher up. There was a glorious chandelier in the middle of the dancing chamber as well, at least fifty feet tall, filled with crystals glistening in the light. The room was large and completely round, and ribbons graced each table with light pink table cloths filled with delicacies for us to try. Chairs were positioned as well for convenient seating. Several musicians played delicate music on harps and mandolins for our dancing pleasure. This was a celebration fit for a king, the commemoration of our apprenticeship.

Looking around, all I could see were the colorful dresses of my colleagues, each a different shade of the rainbow it seemed. Elizabeth's dress was deep salmon and she wore a feathery mask, while Tiffany's was a forest green color. My own was quite beautiful too, in my opinion. It was probably my favorite gown— a deep ocean blue with glitter that created a noticeable trail behind me. I feel sort of bad, because the sparkles are pretty hard to get off of furniture, fabric, people... but that didn't stop me from wearing it. And I wore silver earrings that glinted in the moonlight as well.

We sat together at one of the tables, along with a few other noblemen and women and waited. Then, Professor Winston came to the front stage where the musicians were to address us. "Welcome, Nobles! Congratulations on the completion of your apprenticeships." We applauded him as he feverishly adjusted his glasses.

"According to our records, all of you are on track and scheduled to pass your training, and be crowned as fully fledged rulers of our provinces. Well done." More polite claps followed this. "So, feast, dance, and celebrate!" At that, the music began playing loudly and the event officially began.

"Ready?" August asked me. By this point, I had already grabbed some honey almond cakes and was munching on them. Politely I wiped the crumbs away from my face with a handkerchief and stood to follow, although I did have my eye on some of the punch. In any case, he looked so handsome in his tux, a wonderful dark suit with fancy buttons that I've always had an affinity for. Who could resist that smile, and the powerful and merciful king he would no doubt turn out to become? I looked forward to sharing this moment with my husband-to-be. I stood up excitedly, stretching my hand out for him to hold so we could dance.

"Wait," he said, smiling.

"What?"

"Here, don't forget your tea." Grinning, he passed me my favorite cinnamon. Gleefully, I kissed his cheek before gulping it down. It had its usual spice but a little something extra that I couldn't put my finger on. I appreciated how he always made it taste so great. Together, we took to the center of the ballroom and positioned ourselves for the start of the next dance. We placed our right palms together carefully and I placed my hand on his shoulder, while he curled his behind my left shoulder. With the down stroke of the harp, we were off in a whirl.

The music played softly in the background, but all I could make out was August's face. He was my anchor in this storm of skirts and frills and lace. He would spin me here and there, then dip me. I stepped on his feet a few times, but that was to be expected. Eventually we gave up the traditional rites and just held onto each other, swaying back and forth together, and twirling around. Finally, I just rested my head on his shoulder, and paused, suddenly feeling a little woozy.

"You're very tired, Bella," he said tenderly to me.

"Yes, I know," I said, smiling and closing my eyes. "But at least now that lets me be close to you." We continued to spin and sway.

"You know," he whispered, "if you're tired, we can get out of here to get you some air."

"What is it?" I asked, looking up at him lazily.

"You'll see," he said, holding on to my hands and leading me away from the center of the ballroom. We made our way out of the dancing chamber, and then he started leading me in the direction of the sleeping chambers. I turned to him and found a way to look up at him, although I don't know why it was suddenly so hard. "August, there's actually something I need to tell you." I managed to make out, clearing my throat to try to clear the fog from my brain.

"What's wrong, Bella?" he asked, a concerned look spreading across his face as he held me close.

"Nothing," I replied, and then paused. "I just... I've wanted so badly to connect to my— my people, and I think I've found a way to do so. But I don't want you to be upset with me as to how I have."

"What do you mean? You could never upset me." Warmly, he hugged me close. But before he could ask me for more clarification, I left his arms to turn instead outside. Then, feeling a little more clear-minded with the fresh air, I let down my hair to free it.

"Bella, what are you doing?" He shook his head, holding onto me again at the waist from behind.

I looked at him, "August... I want to go to the Melindan festival tonight... with you!"

"Oh Bella, are you sure about that?" He asked me, pulling me in and beginning to kiss my neck. I felt a mix of elation and confusion. But then panic also set in, because I didn't really have a say in what was happening. At that moment, running footsteps crunched from behind us.

"I brought your cloak, Arabella!" Alex said, laughing as he appeared. And then, he stopped in his tracks, seeing August basically eating my face off. His smile dropped. August drew back from me, and his grip around my waist tightened. I don't think I had ever seen him so upset in my life. With what energy I had left, my eyes grew wide with fear.

"August, I..." but, suddenly weakness overtook me, and I felt my body go limp in his arms. Barely conscious, I could hear Alex yelling for guards.

That's when another character emerged quickly from the

ballroom. "August," Professor Winston said sternly, "step away from the princess."

Disgusted, he looked him up and down. "You really think you can talk to me that way, book boy?"

"Yeah, he can!" Alex began, revving up now. "Why do you ask?"

"Because I'm about to be in charge of you all!" he retorted, letting go of me and rushing towards Alex. Weakly, I fell to the ground immediately, unable to control my limbs. I looked up at them desperately from the dirty ground.

"WHAT DID YOU DO TO ARABELLA?" Alex screamed, lunging himself at August as they began tousling on the ground. Professor Winston went over to help, but August had him knocked out in a moment with a point-blank punch in the face. A few seconds later though, Alex had him pinned to the ground, his legs wrapped around his body, trapping him. "Drug her again, and it will be the end of you," he whispered to him, with a fist looming threateningly above his perfect face. All I could do was watch and blink slowly.

At that moment, the guards appeared and, seeing Alex on top of August, yanked them apart. Uncle Jacob ran over with them. I stayed on the ground, holding myself.

"Well?" Uncle Jacob asked, demanding an explanation from them. For some reason, the guards refrained from picking up my limp body, and instead helped Professor Winston. Luckily, Crystal followed them outside, probably sensing danger with her bodyguard skills. Seeing me, she rushed over and, starting to pick me up and gather my skirts. I appreciated the dignity.

"This man has been dishonoring my fiancé," August said,

between clenched teeth. "He was about to make off with her into the Melindan forest!" At this, I watched weakly as the guards wrestled the two of them apart. Then, August came over to me and gingerly picked me up. I pulled myself away from his reach.

"Get off," I managed to make out, wrestling against his grip, but couldn't seem to get free.

"She's delirious from whatever he's used on her," August explained to the guards, holding me more tightly. "Just give us a moment together so I can—"

But he was cut off. "Both of you, step away from the princess!" one of the guards yelled, pulling him off of me. *Finally,* I thought. *Security being of some good use around here.* Crystal soon had me wrapped around her shoulder and struggled to help me stand. But then they began arresting *Alex*!

"No!" I whispered to her, blinking slowly. "He is not the one who was attacking me!"

"You wouldn't turn me in, love" August hissed to me narrowly. My eyes widened, looking at his own, filled now with such an intensity that I had never seen before. My heart sank, beginning to break in that moment. All I wanted was for us to be together. Between heavy eyes, I looked at his mesmerizing green ones. All I needed to do was consent. Just let Alex be taken away. Fall back into August's perfect, strong arms, even if he did try to take advantage of me. Have the wedding of my dreams, the life my parents expected of me. Thin my brown-skinned bloodline, produce heirs and make everyone happy. *How could I give that up? Wasn't it better than living alone as a disgrace and a failure forever?* At that moment, I closed my eyes, and not just because of whatever was in that tea. A tightness forming in my chest. I knew what I needed to do, but didn't feel strong enough to do it.

"Bella?" he said again to me, lifting my chin to gaze into his eyes, before Crystal could shoo him away. I let out a weak cry, and then—

"NO!" I screamed, pulling myself away from him, mustering what I had left of my consciousness. "Guards this is the man who attacked me!" I pointed at August.

"You Mello!" he shouted, slapping me across the face and sending me tumbling to the ground. In a moment, the guards were on top August.

Alex, free from the guards, ran over to me, and picked me up in his arms, shielding me from any more abuse. I muffled my face in his shoulder, trying to ignore the pain searing across my cheek, and starting to shake as I wept bitterly. As they bound August and dragged him away, I could hear him still shouting out to me. "Arabella! Arabella Bysentor, look at me. Don't do this, Bella! LOOK AT ME! I LOVE YOU! ARABELLA!!" Then he was muffled by the guards and taken away. Still with my eyes closed, I felt a deep abyss forming in my stomach somewhere. Suddenly, Alex's arms felt far away, and then... everything went black.

21

Home

Soft, white rays kissed my face and cheeks, giving me a warm awakening. I opened my eyes slowly, feeling content. But as I blinked more, to my great surprise, I realized I was home. Quickly, I sat up and discovered I was in my own bed and room.

"The princess is awake!" Anne called out. I guess some things are the same then, I thought to myself. At this, I heard a light knock at the door.

Confused, I asked, "Um, who is it?"

"It's me, silly!" an excited voice squeaked back.

"Crystal?" I exclaimed. At that, the door flung open and in she came, all fluffed up with a beautiful light pink gown and tight curls all around her head. Yep, it was her.

"Hey, how are you?" she asked me, sitting at the bottom of my bed and reaching out for my hand, a concerned look spreading across her face now.

"Crystal, wha— how did I, how did you—"

"Shhh," she replied emphatically. "Too many questions at

once!" she giggled, shaking her head, but then stopped, look-ing very serious now. "Are you okay? I never liked that boy, you know."

"What? You helped us get together; you were *rooting* for us!"

"He was always a stuck-up jerk," she replied, shaking her head with disappointment and letting out a huge sigh. "It doesn't really matter now anyway, they're going to behead him, you know."

I was very quiet now. I could have guessed as much. I looked out the window, clutching my night-gowned knees to my chest now. "I really loved him, you know." I said softly. She was silent.

"But—"

"But *what*, Crystal? We were engaged to get *married!* " I chucked a pillow at the wall, watching it singing with my heat as my frustration swelled. "Ugggghhh, how could I have ever thought—"

"Thought what?" she said, getting indignant herself now. I think she began tearing up, but I didn't care.

"That he loved me? That we'd be together?" I threw an-other pillow. Ashes started forming as the pillows were oblit-erated on the floor. "That I'm WORTH SOMETHING?!"

"Stop," she said, tears beginning to fall down her cheeks.

"WHY?!" I asked, raising my voice higher. "Does it make you UNCOMFORTABLE to see me angry? Well, I'm sorry you had to see this!" I yelled. "This was probably my ONE shot to figure things out, to find someone who would tolerate a Mello like me!" Another pillow vaporized before our eyes then.

"No, Bella, you're wrong," she said. "You're one of the most loving people I have ever met, and you have to believe that. You will find real love someday."

"That's real easy for you to say, Crystal!" I shot back.

She shook her head slowly. "No," she said, more decisively this time. "He didn't deserve you, Bella. You are a beautiful person worthy of love and respect because you are human. August was not able to see that." She looked down for a moment. "He's the one that should be crying, Bell, because he's about to get what he deserves." She stopped, looking at me feeling all miserable.

At that, she threw her arms around me decisively. I wept. I just sat there crying in her arms and feeling safe with her, basically my sister at this point, just being with me while I let it out. I cried out my pain, my heartbreak, my fear of being alone, my frustration. I cried out my shame for feeling so worthless, so hopeless.

Without feeling much better, I got ready to face my parents and answer their questions. And I was indebted to have Crystal with me, so I wouldn't have to face their criticism alone. But when I arrived at the chamber, instead of endless interrogation, I was met by my father's steady embrace. We stood there for a good minute just hugging, until we were both ready to let go. The meal was a great relief for me, as I focused on updating my parents about the positive elements of the apprenticeship, the things I had learned and the friends I had made. My mother, who was quiet and reserved as usual, still asked questions, but at least they did not feel accusatory.

"And how did you and Crystal get acquainted?" she asked me.

Crystal and I looked at each other, beginning to laugh. "We met the first day, and sort of just became friends from there. And then we made friends with another noble, Alex, who—"

"Rescued you from the dog, August. Yes, we know," she finished.

"Oh, well, yes. I really learned a lot from them. But, Mother, why haven't Crystal and I been acquainted before the apprenticeship?"

"Well..." she began, "There is something of a potentially complicated relationship with your—"

"Uncle Jacob!" I shouted out. He was coming into the chamber at that moment!

"Yes, yes, hello my Dear!" he said to me, bowing as he entered, his floppy hat always leading the way.

"Jacob," My father began, clearing his throat. "We were not expecting you so early before the coronation."

"Oh, goodness me!" he replied. "Where are my manners? But, there must be some plan for the king's brother, yes?" At that, he placed himself at our table and signaled for a plate to be brought to him.

"Of course, Jacob!" my father exclaimed with a hearty laugh, stretching out his arms. "There will always be a place for you here, brother."

"Wait," I interjected. "Did you just say... coronation?!" I whipped my head frantically between my uncle, father, and mother, waiting for an answer. Finally, Mother cleared her throat.

"According to your reports, your uncle believes you have completed your training in an exceptional manner and should be crowned as quickly as possible," my mother stated matter-of-factly. My eyes grew so wide and my mouth opened wide into a huge grin. Swiftly I turned to Crystal, as if I was about to burst.

"Wait," Crystal interrupted, "My Queen, when is this coronation supposed to take place?"

"Naturally in a week, of course," she replied, shrugging her shoulders and taking another sip of her drink. Looking up, she added, "That's about how long it will take for us to decorate the coronation room and get everything together." Now turning her gaze to me, she gave a warm smile. "Congratulations, Arabella."

I could not hold in the excitement any longer nor believe what I was hearing. Together, Crystal and I let out twin squeals and I quickly stood up and hugged my mother. She eventually consented, beginning to laugh a little herself and hugged me back. Crystal made it into the group hug somehow too. "Yes, Dear, you've done very well and you deserve it," she replied, placing a hand on my shoulder and her face beaming with joy.

"Daughter you must tell us whom you would have as your guests to come to the coronation," Father added. "Of course the entire kingdom is invited, but is there anyone you would like to have in your special party?"

"Yes, Father! Crystal here, Alex from my apprenticeship, and probably a nice... family I met during my project," I added the last part uneasily. I really wanted them to come but it could be challenging to convince my parents that that was a good idea.

"From your project?" Uncle Jacob chimed in. "Why you couldn't mean—"

"Melindans. Yes, actually I do mean them," I replied, finishing his thought for him and holding my chin up high. In that moment, I made up my mind to defend their right to attend my coronation. *How could change come any other way?*

"You met these subjects during your apprenticeship, Daughter?" my father asked.

"Yes. Actually, they were the main reason for a lot of my success. They mentored me as only a grandparent could." I swallowed hard, admitting this out loud. "I owe it to them to join us."

"Very well," my father replied. "We will make sure an invitation is sent to them at once, and expedited."

"Oh yes," Uncle Jacob chimed in gleefully, "We'll make sure they get the message loud and clear."

22

Prison

The following days became something of a whirlwind. Measurements for the new crown, logistics for the after party, invitations to the coronation itself— everything was beginning to come together. I appreciated the distraction it all brought me from the one person I needed to forget entirely— *August*.

Oftentimes, in the middle of answering questions about what decorations I wanted in the ballroom, which food I wanted to eat, and what color I wanted my dress to be, I would stop and think of him. *What if I was planning a wedding right now instead of a coronation?* That's what I should have been doing... if what we had was actually love. *What did we have though? Was it all an illusion, or did we actually feel something?* I know I did, and the way he *looked* at me alone... Well, it certainly felt real and like he wasn't faking it.

I knew I needed to speak to him— to find out the truth of what was happening and what had persuaded him to act this way. *What if he was being set up? What had Peila said about those who don't like Melindans? What if they were the ones behind it?* I needed to think.

The gazebo outside found itself housing me again, its familiar white lilies in full bloom with the sun always blinking back at me. I sang my conflicting feelings out to the only one who seemed to be able to listen impartially — to my mandolin— in the form of the only other lullaby my late grandmother had taught me.

Oye nani, Mana
Oh goodness, my dear
Qua fu eye li
What will we do?
Re lili fu ye sehu
All my friends are with me
Poye rubi ne tu
But I am still alone.

Sitting there, bending over and pouring out my sadness, I felt a little more at peace. The confusion and hurt of the past few days weighed me down deeply, and I searched myself for something to end my pain and fear. Eyes too dry to cry more stung as I kept strumming, hoping for an answer. That's when a solution came to me, but even I could hardly approve of it. Still, I knew it was the one thing that would tell me what I needed to know. Without hesitating, I got up immediately and went to my chambers, swinging the doors shut behind me. There would be no consultation of this plan, otherwise someone might try to stop me.

As much as it made my heart beat uncomfortably, I willed myself to speak not even to Crystal. She of all people would persuade me out of it. I smiled weakly, thinking of her. She was the kindest friend I ever had, always trying to protect me, and always looking out for my best interests. But this was no time for sentimentality. That would have to wait until I was safely crowned queen. I would wait until midnight to make my next move. I was headed to the dungeon for questioning.

It was at least two in the morning before I dared myself to move from my chambers. It was imperative that everyone in the castle was asleep. Carefully, I pulled on my familiar outfit from my runs to the island, and not without my cloak to disguise me. Wait!

I stopped in the mirror and looked myself hard in the eye. I knew I could still be recognized. Resolved, I took a few heavy duty hair ribbons and pulled my curls into neat submission at the nape of my neck, covering my head with my large brown hood now. *Better, much better.*

Satisfied with my disguise, I slinked out of the room and into the hallway, letting the moonlight pouring in from the windows light my path. I didn't even carry a weapon, for fear that I might draw attention I certainly didn't want. Luckily, my hands were good enough weapons if there were trouble.

I made my way down the long corridor in the opposite direction of the breakfast chamber, until at the very end, there was a hard left turn that led to a thin metal door. Opening it slowly, it creaked a little. Refusing to risk making any more noise, I slipped my body through the crack after whipping my head back to make sure no one was watching, pulling my cloak tighter around my face.

Descending down the dungeon, the walls gradually changed from brick and stone to the jagged edges of a cave wall. The only lights down there were the torches precariously nailed to the walls. Their flaming glow bloomed only but so far in the dark cave. Prisoners didn't deserve the light in Promynthia. Seeing extra sticks at the cave-like entrance, I borrowed one already flaming, and made my way deeper into the dungeon.

Passing other prisoners, I felt fear begin to creep up within me, but glancing towards them, I realized most of them were asleep. Feeling a little better, I let myself breathe. But there was one prisoner who was ready to meet me, and was already waiting, as if he knew I would come for him. Suddenly, I felt shamefully predictable, but pushed my self-doubt down. This was no time for such feelings. I needed answers.

August was standing with one tall arm leaning against the bars, his other gripping the columns that trapped him in. "Hey, Bell," he began, looking intently at me. "Miss me much?"

"Listen," I said in a low voice, "I don't want any trouble—"

"Of course not," he cut me off. "So why are you here? To spend the night?" My cheeks reddened, thinking of the forced kiss we had shared.

"Why did you do it?" I asked, ignoring his question.

I saw his handsome features harden into a hard line. A line of straight anger. "You are my bride. I can do as I please with you. I've done nothing wrong."

I let out a half-laugh. "I am no such thing. You do not own me, Frederick IX." He rolled his eyes, reaching out for my shoulders. Quickly, I drew back, and in a reflex, my hand filled with fire and my teeth gritted in defense, ready to burn. He stopped.

"Well then, it looks like you have the stuff to be a real Melindan witch, now don't you?" he commented, his features now being alighted by my light. "Why are you pretending to need that fire stick?"

"August, I have half a mind to let them kill you for what you've done. Tell me why I shouldn't let them," I demanded, throwing the stick to the ground and letting my own flame grow bigger.

He looked me up and down quickly. "Because you're afraid you're a monster," he said calmly, looking straight into the fire I'd created. I tried to stay strong, trying to ignore my now trembling hand.

"You were there when I told them the story," I whispered, tears forming in my eyes now. He turned his green-eyed gaze to me, although in this lighting, they were more golden. His long nose and chin pointed down, darkness surrounding him except for my flame, he looked like more of a dragon. "You don't want the heir of Walabe to suffer at the hands of the new queen, the 'Flame Witch.' The people would never, excuse my joke, warm up to you. *I'm* your act of mercy, Bella."

Silenced, I stood there, my heart filling with anger, and I let my flame go out. I knew that he was right, that this could be just the thing to make the people trust me, to keep the will of my family alive.

Taking a deep breath, I looked at him head on. "I will make sure that you are banished, rather than killed. You can live outside of Promynthia, in the Barren Land, with your crimes and never return."

"I knew you'd see it my way. And now that it's dark..." he replied, reaching out his hands to caress my face. Quickly, I caught his hands in my own, and began to let them burn.

"You will leave the day I am crowned, and *never* return."

With that, I let go of him, my coat twirling to keep up with me, and left without another word.

23

Coronation

The preparations for the coronation only sped up, but thankfully, so did my mind. After talking with the wretch I had once called fiancé, my conscience was finally free to focus on the details of the day I'd been waiting for. I actually began to enjoy the process, and for once, my mother and I seemed to be bonding.

"You like this dress, yes?" She asked me, while they were fitting me in it. My body was somewhat lost in the heaps of shimmering gold fabric they were placing and pining all around me and pinning into place. It seemed the dress was being created before my very eyes. For the convenience of the seam workers, I was gingerly placed atop a sturdy stool so they could make their creation. I appreciated that they gave me a wide and tall mirror to see myself fully, although admittedly it didn't have to be that tall to get all of me in it.

My mother beamed at me, clearly filled with honor at the sight of her daughter being a success. "Arabella, I'm so proud of what you've accomplished, what you've done in this apprenticeship."

"Thank you, Mother."

"I can't wait for you to be able rule with us! You will make a great queen someday."

My heart melted. "You really think so?"

"Just look at yourself," she replied, gesturing towards the mirror. I dared take another peak, and was amazed by the sight that met my eyes. My hair was curled into crisp ringlets down to my shoulders, the gown's shimmering fabric shone in the reflection, and thick sweeping sleeves swaggered my shoulders. The sunlight from the top window beamed in, and gave the entire room a powerful, glittering glow. I looked almost... beautiful, and felt beautiful, too. I smiled at myself.

Mother placed her hand softly to the small of my back and joined me in the reflection. Her own beauty matched my own, but was slightly faded, just because of age. But it didn't change her absolute majestic nature and mesmerizing bouts of wisdom. Her own graying hair was heaped atop her head and a few wrinkles graced her cheeks. I could see how I would become her in thirty years' time. Yet, I wasn't prepared for what happened next. My eyebrows wrinkling in confusion, I peered into the mirror to realize that she was *crying*? I turned to her. "Mother?"

"It's alright, Dear," she reassured me. "I simply am overcome with happiness right now." I looked at her wonderingly. I don't think I had ever seen her shed a tear, let alone bleed. She continued, wiping the few tears that had fallen to her cheeks away. "I love that we are not being erased, but rather celebrated, Arabella. You are showing our people that everyone can be equal." I felt warmth welling within me, so contented at this moment, and so grateful for the woman before me, who had guided me through so much in navigating this white Promynthian world.

"Thank you for all you've done, Mother," I whispered to her, not caring that I was messing up some of the fabric. She held me close.

"Of course, *Mana*."

I pulled away, looking at her in wonder.

"Oh," she began, her cheeks getting warm. "I forget myself and speak of the old ways!"

"It's okay... *Mana*," I replied, winking. Her eyebrows scrunched in confusion, but she accepted it, pulling me in for a much needed heart-filled embrace.

A few days later, the coronation was finally upon us. I woke up that morning, feeling more hopeful than ever before. Today was a new day, a great day to be crowned a ruler of my kingdom. Anne didn't even have to wake me up or to convince me to bathe today— I was way too excited for the day's events. After a quick breakfast, it was time to get dressed for the ceremony. Before I knew it, my maids had me prepared and ready to go.

Taking a final glance at myself in the mirror, I smoothed down the front of my dress taking a slow, deep breath. Today was the day to make history for our country and for myself. Silently, I rehearsed the words that I would say to address the country for the first time as princess, thinking about how I would explain my act of mercy to them. I closed my eyes to try to steady my nerves for a moment, before turning to head out of the door. It was time.

Silently, with servants behind me to assist me with my huge train and Anne leading our mini procession, we traveled down the familiar hallway and headed for the coronation ballroom. I smirked to myself a little, glancing up at the portraits as I continued down the hall. *Maybe I did have what it took to rule this place, even if I looked a little different. And who knew? Maybe mixing things up was a good thing.*

In any case, the appearance of the inner room caught my breath once we arrived. The pews were filled with approving subjects happily awaiting me. Ribbons and sashes adorned about every corner of everything, and the red, velvety carpet was clearly freshly steamed. Other than that, the people themselves were adorning the place, what with their laces and frills and colors ranging from lilac to periwinkle to burnt orange. There were more hat variations than I had ever seen before, and more tulle than I thought existed. I took it all in, waiting patiently for my cue to enter, and took another deep breath. There was no turning back now. If Uncle Jacob said I was ready, then I was ready.

And so it began. "Announcing Miss Arabella Amelia Bysentor of Promynthia!" the officiator boomed over the audience, his voice echoing off the acoustic, wooden walls. My back straightened up a little more. I entered in with the downbeat of the music. A thousand eyes turned to meet my own, some filled with glee and others sober, in full respect.

Trumpets sounded loudly, and my maids and I began our walk down the aisle. I smiled as gracefully as I could, nodding at the crowd, taking steady steps, and trying as much as possible not to be startled by the roses audience members were tossing my way for good blessings. Carefully stepping over them so I wouldn't crush the beautiful things, I finally made my way to the front of the room. I turned to my maids, nodding at them and allowing them to sit now. Then, I made my way up the two steps so I could be at the altar, where the officiator and my Father and Mother stood, awaiting my presence.

"Today is a glorious day and a new chapter for the Bysentor family!" the priest began. "Arabella Amelia has completed her training successfully and is ready to be crowned as your princess." A gentle clap went up from the audience— much different from the whoops and cheers at the Melindan dance— but nonetheless encouraging. He turned to me, outstretching his arm with a jolly, but polite smile. "Come, child," he directed, beckoning me closer, while turning to grab a shiny silvery tiara on a deep purple, velvet pillow. Violins began playing softly in the background to signify my transition to power, and I smiled when I recognized a mandolin playing amongst them.

Gingerly, I stepped towards him and then turned around slowly to face my subjects. As soon as I did, I eyed the crowds and found Crystal and Alex in the second pew, smiling and giggling and waving frantically. Well, to be exact, *Crystal* was the one doing all that. Alex just sat there with a half grin that could have said, *I knew you could do it.* I appreciated them both, and grinned in response. Except, I did note that Peila and Rupert never made it. *Maybe they never got my message?*

"With this crown," the priest continued, lifting my sparkling tiara above my head, "I signify Arabella Amelia as your new ruler. She will have as much power as the King and

Queen, and will be the official predecessor when their time comes to pass this earth." Closing my eyes, I let him place the jeweled prize amongst my curls.

More polite applause followed this, and I curtsied to my new subjects, elated at this truly perfect day. Buoyed up by excitement, I decided to address them immediately.

"People of Promynthia!" I boomed. Everyone quieted immediately and gave me their attention. This felt incredible. *This power at sixteen?* I couldn't believe it was mine. I cleared my throat. "As my first action as your Princess, I would like to declare my act of mercy towards Augustus Frederick IX." Multiple gasps went up from the crowd, including my mother. I ignored her and continued, holding my hands up to request silence. "After much deliberation, I have decided that he is to be exiled rather than put to death for his crimes against the crown. Therefore, I will—" But I was cut off by someone in the fourth row.

At that moment, a white cloaked figure stood up, and peeled back his hood to reveal *August*. Somehow, he was out of his cell.

24

Draw

"I'm not going anywhere, Bella," he spat. Drawing his sword and pointing it at me, he looked completely off kilter and even, insane, what with his unkempt hair now flowing to his shoulders. *Was this even real?* Multiple people began screaming. Some guards started running towards him, but then others in the crowd started... fighting our men. My eyes widened with fear. *Why were people in the crowd against our guards?*

But there was no time for thinking right now. I needed to protect my people. "Drop your weapon!" I shouted at the creep.

He grinned. "You're cute when you're angry."

"*Oye nani!*" I exclaimed angrily. "Just shut up!" His smile not leaving his twisting face, he advanced slowly, sword in hand and ready to fight. I felt panic realizing my hands were just itching to throw flames in his face. *Did I really want the whole country to see what I really was?* I wasn't sure they were ready for that. Thinking quickly and whipping my head back,

I saw some armor on the wall behind me. *Perfect.* I dashed for it. Lugging it before me, I hoisted it up and pointed it in his direction. Eyebrows furrowed down, he continued advancing.

My mind screamed with adrenaline rushing through my veins, but I begged myself to focus on August's body still coming towards me now. If there was one thing I had learned from sparing Godmother, it was never to rush at your opponent head on. I bared my feet into the ground and steadied myself. All of the noise of the guards and the screaming crowds left my brain. All I could see was that once-angelic face rushing towards me. He yelled as he approached within a foot of me—which is when I quickly side-stepped him to the right. At the last moment, I lit the sword in flames and swung it *hard.* Effective, but not enough to make a huge scene. He was knocked to the ground. I looked down at him, watching the deep, singing blow I had dealt him bleeding now from his rib.

He spit on the ground. "Now Bella, why would you do that?" he whined, looking up and showing me his bloodied hand which was pressed against his side. I widened my eyes, shocked by what I had just done to him. Using that moment of uncertainty, he jumped up in a flash and was soon on top of me, pressing his hands dangerously close to my throat, and pinning me to the ground. He snickered darkly, pleased that he had me trapped in his grasp once again. "Do you really want to hurt me, Arabella? I thought you *loved* me?" he mocked. My heart pounded, looking into those eyes turned wild, his face cocked to one side, and flushed with fresh anger. In a moment, he had almost completely cut off my oxygen, pressing the life out of me.

"This... is my... kingdom." I managed to make out, scratching at the hands at my throat. Panic set in for a moment, as I fought to say more to keep drawing in precious oxygen. But then, I remembered Peila's training. *Don't talk, just fight.* Concentrating my panic into action, I reached for his eyes and let the heat flow straight from me. Screaming out in pain, he let go of me and crouched on the ground, rolling and gripping his head in his hands. Quickly, I rolled over and stood up, grabbing my sword quickly with both hands and pointed it steadily at him.

"We're taking over, Princess," he said under his breath. "We're already in control."

At that, I suddenly became aware of my surroundings. Arms still outstretched with my sword, I stole a look at the coronation room. All around me, our soldiers were fighting soldiers dressed in all white, whom I suddenly recognized as the same ones from not only the attack on Walabe, but even the first night I was attacked in the Melindan tavern. My stomach twisted realizing they were there plotting against us the whole time.

By this point, the entire room had been cleared of commoners. I squinted my eyes when I realized, amidst the scuffling, my Uncle Jacob sat calmly in the pews, as if watching the latest drama play as a common spectator.

"Uncle?" I called out to him from across the room.

He slowly turned his head to face me, a dark smirk beginning to curl the corners of his mouth upwards, as if waiting for this moment all along. "It's *King* Bysentor, to you, girl!" he replied.

I stammered, tears beginning to form in my eyes as I began to process. "But... Uncle—"

But he cut me off. "Quiet, *Mello*." Memory shot through me. A blurry and windy night. A dark cloak. A hooded figure looming over me and threatening to throw me off the cliff. But just as my parents and the guards arrived to rescue me, he whipped his head back to see them, and his hood flew off, revealing... my Uncle Jacob. He was behind this the whole time, and he had a limp to prove it from when I'd thrown him off that cliff. The soldiers, the attacks, the apprenticeship, the boy, probably even this coronation. They were all his attempts to take over our kingdom. To destroy me.

I looked back up at him and our eyes locked. He gave a sinister grin, knowing that I now knew the truth. Satisfied by this transfer of knowledge, he yelled out to his swath, "KILL THEM ALL!" Multiple white cloaked soldiers rushing towards me, but our guards rushed too, holding them back. I screamed in terror and fled to the stage. Suddenly, Professor Winston came sprinting in, tripping a little over his fancy coronation robes. And behind him were four silvery horses galloping behind obediently.

"Thank you!" I whispered, unfallen tears now blinding my gaze. At least now I knew he was on my side this whole time. My parents ran over to us now, dodging the soldiers lunging for them and joining us in our circle of protection. They had a few bruises beginning to form around their faces and arms. My jaw dropped, me being amazed that anyone would dare lay a hand on my parents.

My mother kissed my forehead. "Thank heavens that you're safe!" Without another word, our loyal guards helped us mount on our horses— Alex and Professor Winston on their own, Crystal and I sharing and my parents on the last.

We rode out of a hidden tunnel in the corner of the coronation room, our beloved soldiers giving us cover. As we exited our home, they turned back to the coronation, and yelled out, probably for the last time of their lives, "Promynthian at heart!"

Soon, we were galloping across the outer bridge. Alex led our train, but I already knew exactly where we were going. To the island. As we swept across the plain towards the forest, I looked back in dismay as I heard screams of panic from inside our palace and watched as robed, white men took the place of our soldiers on our castle roof. I thought of our servants, our helpers, our maids, and Julian, all trapped. I vowed to return and free them.

Snapping me out of my thoughts, a high whistling sound pierced the air and grow louder. Suddenly, searing pain punched me in the right shoulder, knocking me off of my horse, right after we'd crossed the bridge. An arrow had pierced my flesh. "Ahhhh!" I yelled out in panic. Professor Winston dropped to his knees and lifted my stiff body back onto the horse. Two more whistling sounds, and my parents met their own worlds of pain. Unlike me, they must have expected it, because they gripped onto their horse steady.

Amidst his pain, my father cried out, "Onward, Alex!" So we continued our desperate quest to the island. During most of that ride, I went in and out of consciousness, blacking out against the pain in my arm.

In what seemed like either three hours or five minutes, we had reached the dock. Peila and Rupert were there to meet us. Of course, they just had that sort of instinct to be there.

But before they could lead our horses up to their home, my mother cried out desperately.

"Arabella!" I shot my eyes back, suddenly completely awake. Adrenaline temporarily cured my wound. I dismounted and ran to them, and held her hand.

"Mother?" I looked at my parents, both slumped lazily against their steed.

"Arabella," she coughed wearily. "We love you very much. But we could only bring you this far."

"Mother, what are you talking about?!" I screamed out, tears beginning to stream down my face. "Father, what does she mean?" I turned to him desperately, wanting an explanation. At that, I saw the arrow sunk deeply into his right side. He lifted his head, and placed a cold hand on my face.

"We've always known you will do great things, Daughter."

"Father!" I screamed, looking at his wound. Panic overtook me, and my breaths became shaky.

"Wait! I think I can heal you!" I tried to begin, holding my hands out to each, but Mother shushed me.

"Arabella, listen to me!" she whispered. "There's not enough time for us, *Mana*." Her address hurt deeply even as it warmed me. I guess she had finally started to accept her roots. Maybe she had never left them behind. She beckoned me look into her eyes rather than at her own deep wound. "You are the rightful heir to the throne."

I blinked back tears, and replied, "Yes, Mother."

"We love you, Arabella," Father whispered.

Mother gripped my hand and pulled me close. "Win back the land... for all of us," she murmured.

"Mother?" I grabbed her clammy hand, gasping for air. I

shot my eyes back towards my father's body, unable to even make out the words. That's when I collapsed to the ground, shaking and crying out to the clay earth. They were gone.

25

Queen

I understood now why Peila and Rupert hadn't come to the coronation. They were never given the message from my uncle. I sat in their home, worn with grief and covered in dirt. It was all I could do to stay staring at the mud floor, my hands feeling my now tattered coronation gown. My tiara sat peacefully on the kitchen table, mended by Rupert's caring hands, but I could hardly look at it. *Is this what I had to pay to be a ruler for my people?*

I wasn't alone for long. Crystal and Alex came in, and just sat with me on the cold hard ground, waiting for me to say... anything. They took turns holding my hand or shoulder. I definitely appreciated their presence. Peila quietly served us food, not beckoning us to come sit or talk like she usually would. She knew it had been quite the ending of the day for me. Professor Winston stayed outside, in respect for their home, and to help answer questions of anyone who might stop by.

I shook my head in disbelief. *How had this happened?* A

coup had taken over the palace, the king and queen were dead, and my former fiancé was living and joined with my corrupt uncle. It honestly just sounded like some bizarre story line to me, yet it was real. Every inch of it, real. And now... I guess that made me the new ruler of Promythia? *But who in the world would listen to a little girl like me? Someone with my skin?* There was no way.

But then I stopped myself. This was *my* kingdom. No one could steal it from me without me letting them take it. The least I could do was to put up a fight. And there was no way everyone in the country wanted to be ruled by these vagabonds. Every day, more and more Promynthians were getting used to Melindans like me in the castle. If we were going to make this change, I guess the time was now or never. With my mind made up, I stood suddenly.

"You okay, Bella?" Crystal asked quietly, concern spreading across her face. Alex too, touched my arm gently.

I nodded at them, grateful for their help. "I think I'm feeling better than I have in a while, actually." Right then, Alex pulled me in for a hug.

"I'm so glad to hear that, Bella," he whispered. Surprised by the warmth, I nestled into the embrace. I don't think I had noticed before how well I fit under his chin before. "You know," he began, pulling back from me but not removing his gentle hands from my shoulders, "I never told you what happened to my parents." I caught my breath as he gingerly wiped away one of my remaining tears with his thumb. This felt like too much. I wasn't ready for a new relationship. Not now, maybe not ever. "Maybe my story could be relatable for—" But I cut him off, shaking my head. Nothing that happened to him could ever compare to my grief. I shook myself loose from his arms. Regret seemed to fill his face, as if he knew he had said too much, revealed too much of his feelings for me in that one gesture.

Before any more emotions could overtake me, I grabbed my tiara, and stepped outside into the fresh air, inhaling its contents deeply. Not surprisingly, the whole town seemed to have gathered on Peila and Rupert's land. They were praying over us, bidding us good will, and waiting to see what had become of the princess. It was time for me to show them. After a quick fluff to my tattered dress I was ready.

I shot up a flame in the sky to get everyone's attention. "My Dear Melindans!" They all turned to me quickly. "I want to thank you for your support today. Thanks to all of you, the entire royal family has not been destroyed, as the Watchers would have it." Cheers went up to the sky. I nodded slowly.

"You all have kept me safe, and hidden me successfully. But the Watchers are not done yet. They will come here to look for us, to destroy us. But," I paused, pulling out a ball of fire and grinning at it, "they will NOT succeed!" The people now were sending up yells of delight and applause into the dimming night sky. "Join me in taking back my kingdom, not just for me, but for all of us. Who is with me?" At that, I held up my golden sparkling hand, as I had done during the night of the Melindan dance. Soon, the entire crowd was following suit, throwing up hands sparkling with different colors, representing whatever they could wield.

I smiled again, glancing at Alex and Crystal, who were just beaming at me, and furrowed my eyebrows to the crowd again, determined to win.

Coming Soon

CONGRATS on finishing the book! Let me know what you thought by leaving a review on Amazon.com where you bought it!

Also, get HYPE, because the sequel is coming soon, so stay tuned. You didn't think I'd leave you with a cliff-hanger, did you? In order to find me and keep up with the next book, be sure to follow me on Instagram and YouTube **@trperrywrites** and see my website at **trperrywrites.net** And, of course, you can find me on Amazon where you got the first book. Finally, if you want my hand-designed MERCH to show off your new *Rose Wielder* support of Arabella, you can find my Etsy shop at **etsy.com** if you type my name in the search bar, **"trperrywrites."**

Seriously, if you liked this book, tag me on Instagram. Share what you thought there and on an Amazon review and let others know to buy it too. *Oye nani,* don't be selfish, tell others!

Okay, I think that's all for now. Sit tight and I'll see you back on the Melindan island soon.

Map of Promynthian Country
drawn by t. r. perry